ONLY ONE BOY

FIRST LOVES #2

MAGGIE DALLEN

Copyright © 2021 by Maggie Dallen

All rights reserved.

No part of this book may be reproduced in any form or by any electronic or mechanical means, including information storage and retrieval systems, without written permission from the author, except for the use of brief quotations in a book review.

Cover by Tugboat Design

❊ Created with Vellum

ONE

Celia

THE CAR COMES to another halting stop as we inch our way toward the train station. My friend Ryan is driving and he flashes me this wince of regret that somehow only makes me feel worse.

"How is there traffic right now?" My voice is so high it sounds like I'm about to cry.

Probably because I *am* about to cry.

My best friend Mara reaches forward from the backseat to rest a hand on my shoulder. "I think it might be time to face the fact that we're going to miss the train."

Just then the traffic ahead of us moves forward, and Ryan accelerates, and...steps on the brake two seconds later as the cars ahead of us come to another grinding halt.

I grip the dashboard of Ryan's car so hard my fingers turn white. "I could make a run for it," I say to no one in particular. It's crazy talk and I know it. There's a major highway separating me from the train tracks, not to mention the fact that I'd be lugging my carry-on through oncoming traffic.

"The backup is coming from roadwork on Dewey Boulevard," he says, pointing to our right—toward the train station. "You'd have to cross through a construction site to reach the highway."

I stare at him and then turn to Mara. "What do I do?"

My uber-competent friend is already in action, frowning down at her phone. "There's another train leaving in ten. You'll have to buy another ticket and it looks like you'll need to transfer, but it'll get you to New York."

I nod, trying to swallow down this panic. I won't be with the rest of the leadership club from my school, but I don't care about riding with my friends nearly so much as I do getting to the city on time.

This presentation is everything to me. The dean of Cornell's business school will be there, and if he's impressed with my speech, I might even be able to score an in-person interview.

Mara is apparently reading my mind because she leans forward again. "The presentation isn't until tomorrow. You have all day to get to New York and it's only a six-hour train ride. You've got this."

I nod as Ryan veers into another lane, trying to inch us closer. It's no use. There's traffic everywhere. Even making the next train seems like a stretch.

Impatience makes it impossible to sit still. It doesn't help that my phone keeps lighting up with texts from Noelle, who's already on the train with our other classmates and asking where on earth I am.

I shoot her back a text. *Running late thanks to traffic. Tell Mr. Deckman I'll be on the next train.*

She shoots back a thumbs up along with a handful of

sad-face emojis.

I go to text back but stop myself. They don't make emojis that adequately express how I feel right now.

But I keep my phone on, the screen facing me. I'm still waiting for my mom to respond to my SOS. Not that it'll help now, of course. But she's the reason I'm in this predicament. The least she can do is acknowledge that she's screwed me over.

It was her car that had issues last week, her car that's in the shop. The fact that she borrowed my car and didn't even stop to consider that I might have planned on using it to get to the most important event of my life thus far is just a tiny bit frustrating.

I draw in a deep, slow breath and let it out through pursed lips like my yoga instructor taught us. Like you're breathing out through a straw, she says. It's supposed to calm me when my nervous system is frayed and my belly is a pit of poisonous anxious toxins.

It's not working. All it's doing is calling attention to how crazy I must seem right now.

Mara's expression in the rearview mirror is one of motherly concern. And even easygoing Ryan is casting worried looks my way.

"Thanks again for the ride," I say, mainly to break the silence before I scream with frustration at the way we're jerking forward so slowly I'm tempted once again to risk my life and my luggage in a mad dash to the station.

"Of course," Mara says.

"We got there as soon as we could," Ryan adds.

"I know and I appreciate it," I say.

I'd already been on the verge of tears when I'd called Mara in a panic, and they'd cut short their morning together to come and give me a lift. It's not their fault I'm in this pickle. It's my fault I'm late because, like a moron, I'd thought maybe my mom would be thinking about me for once.

It had taken me too long to realize my mom wasn't at home. Even longer to realize she'd taken my car. And then I'd waited for way too long for her to reply to my texts and calls asking her to come back and give me a lift.

Nope. There's only one person to blame for this morning's epic fail, and that person is me.

I look over to see Mara and Ryan wearing matching looks of frustration and irritation. They're two of the most competitive, driven people I know. It must be killing them that they failed in their mission to get me to the train station.

But that's how this whole field trip has been panning out. I'd been joking for weeks now that this trip is cursed, and this morning's debacle is just the latest example. As the president of the club, nothing had gone right during the planning. There were issues getting approval from the school board, then the fundraiser to help pay for the trip hadn't raised as much as we'd hoped, and then there were the last minute cancelations, which had us scrambling to fill the spots so we could meet the requirements, followed by hiccups with the hotel reservations, and...

I let my head fall back against the headrest with a sigh. Thinking about all the ways this trip has felt doomed from the start is so not helping right now.

I try to count the number of cars ahead of us instead. Although, what I should be doing is rehearsing my speech. That's another issue that came up over the last few weeks. I'd been planning on doing a joint business innovation presentation with my friends Noelle and Elijah, but then Mr. Deckman and I found out about the dean from Cornell being on the panel of judges and in a rush of confidence that is nowhere to be found at the moment, I'd declared that I was going to do a solo presentation on top of the joint one already planned.

Like a bolt of lightning, I'd been struck with this awesome idea for the business start-up category, and I'd been working around the clock to bring it to fruition. Mr. Deckman loves it, and I do too, but the problem is, I now have a ten-minute speech to memorize *and* I have to be able to answer any questions they might throw my way.

So, basically, I've gone and made an already stressful school event approximately eight hundred times more stressful.

Way to go, me.

Mara and Ryan are murmuring quietly to each other now, and from what I can make out they're coming up with a plan C and a plan D in case this new plan B of catching the next train doesn't work.

I force a sigh out through an imaginary straw. This trip is *not* doomed...but not even my favorite power couple could make this morning run smoothly.

"Almost there," Mara says behind me. She's starting to sound as nervous as I feel.

I smooth a hand over my hair as the station comes into view. By 'almost there' she means we still have a huge thoroughfare to cross through. So close, yet so far away. But I pull down the visor and check my reflection as if I'll be jumping out any second now.

Despite the crazy, harried, frazzled wreck I am on the inside, I'm not a mess on the outside, so that's something. My long brown hair is still smooth and flat, my lipgloss hasn't been entirely gnawed off yet, and a glance down at my still-perfect manicure inexplicably makes me feel better.

Not by much, but the pretty, pink nails work better to calm me than the breathing-out-through-a-straw technique ever has, so I'll take it.

A half a million stops and starts later, we finally reach the station. Ryan's out in a flash and has my rolling luggage out of the trunk and on the sidewalk before I've even shut my passenger side door behind me.

I'm normally a hugger, and I owe these two way more than a quick wave as I grab my luggage and run, but we all know I don't have time for long, drawn-out goodbyes.

"Good luck!" Ryan shouts.

"Call if you need anything!" Mara adds.

I throw my free hand up in a parting wave but don't spare a glance back as I dive into the chaos that is the Lakeview train station in our little Upstate New York town that borders Lake Ontario. Not that Lakeview is named after *that* massive lake. Oh no. We're named for the much smaller, but no less picturesque lake in our town that brings a fair share of tourists during the summer and the fall.

Although, I'm pretty sure most of the tourists who come here during this time of year are here for the changing leaves, something I normally love as well. But right now I have no patience for the leaf-peepers climbing out of the train.

With a quick glance at the board overheard, I see it. Final destination is Grand Central.

I let out a long exhale as relief floods through me. Finally, something is going right. I bound onto the train and only then stop to think about the fact that I don't have a ticket.

I'd bought my ticket for the last train a month ago but they had to sell tickets on board too, right?

Probably?

A few stragglers jostle past me to exit as I make my way through the crowded train. Row after row, I smile politely at the blank stares that turn in my direction.

I spot a conductor heading in my direction. The sour look on his face says he's in no mood for small talk so I refrain from bombarding him with a million questions and hand over my mom's credit card, which is to be used for emergency purposes only.

But if this doesn't qualify as an emergency, I don't know what does. And besides, it's her fault I'm in this mess so I have zero qualms handing over the slip of plastic and I watch as he slides it through his portable ticket processor. He hands me a little stub as a receipt and nods toward the front of a train. "Not many seats open, but you can try."

I smile and thank him before heading for the front. I keep smiling as I hit the next car where the passengers are facing in my direction so I feel like a model on a catwalk as I make my way down the aisle in my pink blouse, pleated skirt, and ballet flats.

Well, a model who's sweating after her mad dash onto the train and who's lugging a roller case behind her in the least graceful way imaginable. "Oops, sorry," I say as the bag catches on a man's briefcase and knocks it over.

"So sorry," I murmur again as my luggage rolls over the toes of a woman wearing a pantsuit. She doesn't stop talking into her phone as she scowls at me.

I give her another apologetic grimace and continue on my way.

There are a few times when I'm sure I spot an empty seat next to someone but get closer only to find that the empty seat is actually filled with either a child or a sleeping passenger who's slumped down so low they're not noticeable until I'm right next to their row.

I was hoping to have a row to myself, to be honest. I typically don't mind sitting next to strangers—I'm an outgoing kind of girl. Always have been the smiley sort, prone to chatting with whoever I'm near. Give me a silence and I'll fill it, that's my unofficial motto.

Well...usually. There's one guy who reduces me to a speechless state whenever he's near, but aside from those awkward run-ins with Heath Reilly, Lakeview High's brooding basketball star, I'm your basic chatty Cathy.

So no, I don't mind sitting next to strangers, in theory, but I'd been hoping to spread out my notecards so I could work on my presentation on the ride.

I smile at an old man who's frowning at me like my presence in this already-crowded train car is a personal affront.

It's clear a row to myself is *not* going to happen. I'll be lucky if I find any seat at all. Will they let me ride standing up? My heart starts to race with worry as I realize how little I know about trains. The last time I was on one, I'd been with my mom and dad when they'd taken me to Boston to see the Icecapades.

That was obviously quite a while ago. And this is so not like that trip.

In the next car I finally spot a seat—if you can call it that. It's actually a little pullout bench across from the luggage storage area. It reminds me of those little flip-down seats flight attendants seem to pull out of nowhere when there's turbulence.

It's small, clearly stowable, and facing a poster with directions on what to do if we see something suspicious. But when I shove my luggage into the corner and take the seat, no one protests and tries to kick me out, so for the first time all morning, I start to relax.

I roll my shoulders back and take a deep, calming

breath. Has this morning gone as planned? No. Not even remotely. But maybe my luck is starting to change. Sure I'll be late, but once I meet up with the others at the midtown hotel, this portion of the trip will all be forgotten.

And until then...

I open the crossbody satchel I'm holding in my lap and pull out my notecards. Until then, at least I'll have plenty of time to memorize and mentally rehearse.

The train gives a little kick and lets out a puff of air like it's about to start moving. That's when the sliding doors separating cars opens right next to me, and that newfound contented feeling? It disappears in a heartbeat.

Heath Reilly is standing there.

I blink and my jaw drops.

Heath Reilly?

No way. Maybe it's just someone who looks like Heath.

I can only see half of his face, so maybe my mind is playing tricks on me. Because seriously, what would he even be doing here? It can't be him.

But there he is, standing in the open doorway and scanning the seats of this car with a frown. He turns his face slightly to take in the seats behind me and I have a clear view of the chiseled jaw, the hazel eyes, the cropped, light brown, permanent bedhead, and those eyebrows that seem to naturally pull together in a frown, like he's forever brooding.

Yup. That's the signature look that cinches it.

There's no doubt about it. This is no doppelganger who bears a striking resemblance.

It's definitely Heath.

My jaw drops further and my eyes widen in horror because...this cannot be happening. What is Heath even doing here?

But even as I think it, my logical brain kicks into action. He's heading to New York. Obviously. For the school trip, most likely. My brain refuses to believe this even though it's the only logical explanation it can muster.

It's self-preservation that keeps me from believing it because...I can't do this. Panic hits me smack in the chest.

I cannot survive a weekend trip with Heath Reilly. Don't ask me how it came about or why, but sometime around second grade I'd realized he's the bee's knees.

Yes, it's a lame expression but it sums up the silly infatuation I'd harbored as a child. An infatuation that turned into an even bigger crush as we both got older and he just kept getting hotter. At the same time, I'd gotten more and more allergic to his presence.

When he's near, I can't think, I can barely breathe—

It's unnatural and it's really bad for my health. But the worst part is, my personality goes flying out the window. I forget how to talk, let alone how to charm or flirt. I don't even know how to smile when he looks at me with those pretty hazel eyes.

Turn around. Turn around and walk away. My attempts at ESP are a fail. Not surprisingly.

He doesn't move, just continues to hover there by the car door like he's waiting for something. Or...someone?

And that's when he spots me. His perusal of the crowded seats has ended with me. His frown turns to a look of confusion. "Celia?"

I try to swallow and choke on my own spit.

Crap on a cracker, I can't even confirm my own name. That I am, in fact, me. Celia Kennedy. The girl he's been going to school with since kindergarten.

The conductor enters our car right behind Heath and I'm temporarily off the hook as Heath turns to talk to the same surly, harried man who'd given me a ticket. I can't hear what they say until the end. Until the conductor gestures toward me and my itty-bitty little foldout seat which, I guess, theoretically, at least, is meant for two.

If those two people were, say, toddlers. It's definitely not meant for two grown individuals...unless they were planning on snuggling for the duration of the trip.

Heath's gaze meets mine and he gives me a little smile that seems strained by the tension that lines his mouth and eyes.

He's as unhappy about this as I am, that much is clear. Though I'm not sure if he's pissed to be stuck next to me or if it's something else.

Also, more importantly...what is he doing here?

A question I should ask, probably, but don't. Instead, I stare up at him like a mute moron as he hovers uncertainly in the aisle. Finally, he glances down at the empty half-seat beside me. "Is this seat taken?"

He's trying for teasing, but I'd bet my mom's credit card neither of us is much in the mood for jokes right now.

I try to say no but settle for a shake of my head instead as I scramble to pick up the cards I'd already set down beside me to give him some room.

No, I try to say.

Have a seat, I think.

None of that comes out of my mouth though because my tongue is roughly twice its usual size and my mouth has gone bone dry.

I can't even blink, let alone smile.

Shock, it seems, only makes my condition worse.

I have no idea why Heath Reilly is on this train bound for New York...but I do know that this day from hell?

It just got a whole lot worse.

TWO

Heath

I CAN'T EXACTLY CLAIM to be the most likeable guy in the world.

I'm not all confident and outgoing like my best friend Ryan, or the charming guy who lives to party like my other friend Elijah. I'm good at basketball but I'm not some driven phenom like some other guys on the team. But even though I'm not super funny or charming or talented, people tend to like me.

Girls tend to like me.

Don't ask me why. I don't get it either. But that's the way it is and that's the way it's always been. I've somehow fooled the students of Lakeview High into thinking I'm...cool, or whatever.

Everyone seems to think so.

Except for *her*.

Celia stares at me as I slide into the tiny space beside her. It's not a good stare. It's the kind of stare that makes me think the cops are gonna be called any second now. If anyone on this train were paying attention, I'd expect to hear sirens as they come to arrest that shady dude who's scaring the crap out of the cute preppy chick.

I try for a smile despite the fact that my morning sucks.

Celia stares back at me with wide, terrified eyes like I'm a kidnapper holding a gun to her side.

So, yeah. Awesome. This day just keeps getting better and better.

I half turn in my seat to do one last sweep of the rows behind me as if my girlfriend Pamela might be playing a game of hide-and-seek.

She's not here. Just like she wasn't on any of the other train cars.

Just like she wasn't at her house waiting for a ride like she was supposed to be.

I sit back with a sigh. Where the hell *is* she?

I turn my attention back to the device in my hand—the stupid, broken piece of crap that I call a phone. I'm currently staring at a black screen so I go to hit the power button on the side.

Sometimes turning it off and on again helps.

I watch it take its sweet time coming to life as the train kicks underneath us and starts to move. I'm painfully aware of the silence next to me and it does nothing for this tension in my chest.

"You missed the train too, huh?" I say.

And yeah... Captain Obvious here, at your service.

"Yes." Her voice is little more than a whisper.

I swear I have no idea what I ever did to this girl to make her hate me, but she does. This much is clear. I've been going to school with her since forever so I know what I'm talking about. We have friends in common, we go to the same parties, take most of the same classes, and through all of that she either goes out of her way to avoid me or pretends I don't exist.

I know very well that Celia is capable of talking. A lot, actually. I hear her chatting away with her friends, cheering at pep rallies and games, flirting with the guys in our class, and laughing at their jokes. I've seen her go out of her way to befriend the new kids, to include the outcasts, to laugh at jokes that fall flat out of kindness...

My point is, Celia Kennedy is fully capable of being an outgoing, chatty little sweetheart to literally *everyone* at our school except for me.

Why? I wish I knew.

Silence falls between us again and I'm still staring at my phone as it does the longest boot-up known to man. It's very possible that this time it won't turn on.

I wince as I stare down at it.

Please don't let this be the day it dies.

The slow way the apps pop up on the screen isn't exactly heartening and the sound it makes is the smartphone equivalent of a death rattle, but I let out a sigh of relief because...it's alive.

Dying, yes. On its last legs, for sure. But it's alive enough for me to make a call.

Pamela answers on the third ring and the second I hear her voice, I know she's pissed. "Heath, what do you want?"

Her words don't exactly hide her annoyance either. I reach up and pinch the bridge of my nose. Why is she pissed?

No idea.

"Where are you?" I try to keep my voice down and hope to hell Celia isn't trying to listen.

The train's wheels on the tracks provide some white

noise, but no one else on this train car is talking at this particular moment. I'm acutely aware that even while speaking in low tones, it feels like I'm shouting next to Silent Celia over here.

I'm even more aware of the silence on the other end of the line.

I move the phone away from my ear to make sure the call hadn't dropped. But it says it's still going and—

"Didn't you get my texts?" Pamela's voice comes out so loud, I jerk back in my seat and I feel Celia jump beside me too.

Crap. I lift the phone back to my ear, my finger seeking out the volume button to try and lower it before she talks again. "What texts?"

She sighs. "It's over, Heath."

I'd hit the wrong volume button.

Her voice is louder than before and I tug the phone away from my ear to save my eardrums, but that means her voice is a loud squawk that everyone can hear.

It's over.

The words seem to ring in the air of this too-quiet train car.

I stare at the phone in my hand like an idiot. The words don't make sense.

They *should*. I've definitely heard them often enough. I've lost track of how many times Pamela has ended things with me over the past two years. Just like I can no longer count how often she's come running back.

She's still talking, saying something about how I can't blame her for moving on. We both knew this relationship was doomed. I want to respond. I have about a million questions because the last time I saw her—two days ago at Noelle's back-to-school pool party—we were fine.

Or...I thought we were fine.

But I can't respond because I'm frantically pushing the volume button to its lowest setting. It's not helping. The volume is going down but her words are still filling the air between me and Celia. For the first time in years, this phone's speaker quality is crystal clear.

Maybe the guy in the back isn't getting all the details but up here at the front of the train car, everyone in the near vicinity can hear my girlfriend giving me 'the talk.'

"I'm just not ready for this kind of commitment," Pamela's saying. "I really thought this time would be different, but—"

"Pamela," I cut in when I finally give up on the volume.

I no longer care about all the questions racing in my head because all that matters is ending this public humiliation.

"What?" She sounds so exasperated. Like I've just called her to harass her or something. Like we've been over this a million times before and she hates having to repeat herself.

Which...I guess maybe we have. But not since our last breakup. Not since she came to me this summer crying, saying she made a mistake. My fists clench. She swore this time was going to be different.

And you believed that?

No. Not really. But I'd still taken her back—again—because...because...

Ah hell, I didn't know why I kept doing this to myself.

I take a deep breath and glance over at Celia, but she's staring fixedly at the scene outside the window. It's just trees flashing by but the way she's staring you'd think she was watching an engrossing movie.

I pinch the bridge of my nose again, but the dull

headache I'd been dealing with all morning is turning into a full-fledged hammering on my skull. "Pamela," I say again quietly, hoping my low, calm voice will diffuse what is going to rapidly turn into an emotional tornado on her end.

Ask me how I know.

"What?" she says again, even snippier than before because I'd been keeping her waiting as I try to figure out how to end this call without being a total jerk. "Why are you even calling?" she continues. "You know I leave for that field trip today."

My jaw drops, because… "You're on the train to New York?"

"Obviously," she huffs.

"I came to pick you up—"

"Why did you do that?"

"Because that was the plan." My voice is rising now despite my best intentions. I'm not yelling, far from it. But frustration gives my tone an edge that Pamela can obviously hear.

"That *was* the plan," she says, stressing the past tense. "But I changed my mind. I…" She lets out a sharp exhale. "Didn't you get my texts?"

Her texts? I move the phone away again to stare at my screen like her texts might magically appear.

They don't.

"No," I bite out through clenched teeth.

"Oh." And then after a heartbeat. "Heath, you really need to get a new phone."

And you really need to stop breaking up with people via text.

"Pamela—"

"Where are you now?" She sounds suspicious. Like I'm

some creeper and not the guy who was her boyfriend up until three seconds ago.

"I'm on a train," I mutter as quietly as possible.

Celia's not turning to face me, but I don't need to see her expression to know she's hearing every word.

Heck, that pantsuit lady halfway back could probably hear every word.

There's another silence on Pamela's end, and I can just imagine Pamela looking around her train. I can picture her long blonde hair swinging as she turns this way and that to find me.

"I'm not on your train," I say. "I missed that train because I was waiting for you."

"And that's *my* fault?" she snaps.

Yeah. It kind of is. But I definitely can't handle having another battle with Pamela here and now. Not when Celia-the-Silent can hear every single word we're saying.

"Look, I gotta go," I start.

I don't get a chance to finish because my phone goes dead and the sudden silence is deafening.

I swear I can feel Celia trying not to make any sound next to me, and her tension only adds to mine.

Pamela just broke up with me. The realization hits me anew now that I'm staring at a once-again blank screen.

It's over between us.

I try to summon up any emotion, but aside from humiliation I got nothin'. I will feel something, I'm sure. But right now, all I can focus on is the fact that this rattly old train is currently carrying me toward New York City—and my ex.

I scrub a hand over my face and take a deep breath as I try to figure out how I'm gonna get out of this. I'm not still gonna go, obviously. But is it too late to get my money back? I've never particularly cared to see New York, and I'd barely been able to afford this trip. My family's not poor, but money in my house is...toxic. Kind of like my relationship with Pamela.

There are always strings attached when I take money from my dad, and if my mom finds out? Forget it. They start fighting. Again. Over everything and anything except what's really bothering them. And voila...whatever tentative peace we have in the house is gone.

I'm old enough to handle it if my mom takes another 'break' or Dad goes back to that other woman he's always threatening to leave my mom for, but my little brothers don't need to go through that again. Not if I can help it.

It's easier to just not ask my parents for anything to keep the peace. Instead, I make do with what I've earned during my summer job and whatever part-time work I can pick up at my uncle's car repair shop during the off-season.

So, basically, I spent all my spending money on a trip to a city I don't care to visit for a girl who just broke up with me over a text.

And oh yeah, the one girl from school who hates my guts just witnessed the whole thing.

Fan-freakin'-tastic.

"Excuse me, sir?" I reach a hand out to hail the conductor as he passes through to check for ticket stubs.

He frowns at me like I just ruined his day.

"Er—" I glance around me. I swear, everyone is staring. Like, *everyone*. Pantsuit lady, the guy with the briefcase, the kid with the tablet and earbuds nicer than mine...

I turn back to the conductor. "Where can I get a train back to Lakeview?"

He stares at me like I spoke Greek.

I'm pretty sure I can feel Celia's eyes on me.

In lieu of a response, the conductor gives an exasperated

sigh that rivals Pamela's in how much it manages to convey his disdain for me, and then he reaches into his uniform pocket and tosses me a tiny pamphlet. I unfold it to see it's a timetable.

Honestly, I'm not sure if it's the rocking of the train, or the way my neck is burning from all the stares aimed in my direction, or the fact that Celia seems to be holding her breath beside me, but I can't make heads or tails of the thing.

I stare at it blankly until the conductor apparently takes pity on me and jabs a finger in the middle of the confusing chart. "You can get a train back when we hit Elmdale."

"Elmdale?" Celia's voice is so jarring, I nearly drop the schedule.

It's not that she was loud, it's just she's been so deathly quiet since I got on board that a whisper from her would be alarming.

I glance over to see she's staring up at the conductor in clear confusion.

"I thought we were going to transfer in Pineview," she says.

The conductor sighs again and gives her a look that has her shifting beside me in discomfort. I can't blame her. He looks disturbingly like our principal right before he's about to give us a lecture on how he expects us to behave during pep rallies.

"This is the local train," he says, leaning forward to jab at another meaningless set of times and numbers. "If you want to get to Grand Central, or go back where you came from—" He shoots me a disgruntled look like I'd intentionally gotten on this train from hell just to annoy him. "Then you're gonna have to transfer at Elmdale."

"How far is…" I trail off because he's already walking

away. I turn back to Celia, but she's hunched over the schedule, apparently trying to decipher the thing.

Since I'm holding it, she's leaning in toward me and I get hit with a wave of peach-scented shampoo as some of her long, straight brown hair brushes against my shoulder.

I don't move.

I kind of...freeze, actually.

Celia has never been this close to me and I'm weirdly afraid I'm going to scare her off if I alert her to my presence.

She makes me feel like the big bad wolf I am most definitely not.

But she acts like I am, so around her I feel that way.

"So, I guess we're stuck here until Elmdale," I finally say when she shifts away from me to lean against the window. Maybe she too just realized how close she'd been because her eyes are wide and stricken, like a deer in headlights as she glances over at me.

"Which is..." I wince as I look down at the jumble of numbers. "How far?"

She takes a deep breath, and I know I'm not imagining her distress when she whispers, "Three hours."

THREE

Celia

THREE HOURS?

My foot starts to tap to the rhythm of the train's rocking as I turn to look out the window.

Three *hours*.

Repeating it to myself doesn't make it any more palatable.

Three hours stuck on this tiny seat next to Heath Freakin' Reilly. Three hours of pretending I didn't just hear him get dumped. Three hours of this painful, awkward silence that's already settling over us like a weighted blanket.

The sunny view disappears as we plunge into a dark tunnel. I flinch at the pitch blackness outside of us.

I hate the dark.

My foot starts tapping faster and I can't even imagine pulling out my notecards to memorize anything. Trying to concentrate when Heath Reilly is sitting next to me is beyond impossible.

So that's it then.

Three more hours of this. Which is basically three hours of unproductive torture.

I grit my teeth in frustration. Seriously. How could this day possibly get any worse?

The train jerks and comes to a halt so suddenly, I let out a squeak. I start to slide off the seat but Heath catches me with an arm across my waist like a well-toned seatbelt.

Everyone on the train is yipping with alarm and shouting out questions, and then—

Snick.

The fluorescent lights inside the train flicker and die.

The noise that escapes me is...not a squeak. I wish it was. This sound is something far more pathetic.

My heart's in my throat as panic slams into my chest. Heath's voice is a low rumble next to my ear. "I'm sure the lights will come back on soon. They have to have emergency lights or something."

I draw in a short breath and I manage a nod. Which is not super helpful considering we're in pitch blackness at the moment.

"Thanks," I whisper.

I can do this. I try to slow my breathing. I can at least pretend to be calm. But I really, truly hate the dark.

Like, it's possible I have a phobia. It's definitely a very real fear.

And that's when I realize I am clawing Heath Reilly. On instinct I'd gripped his arm which is still cinched around my waist and my pink, perfectly manicured nails are currently digging into his forearm. I let go with a gasp. "Sorry."

I'm still whispering and I don't know why. Lord knows no one else is—the other passengers are shouting out questions and talking loudly to one another.

It seems Heath and I are the only ones sitting in silence.

Awkward silence.

Wow. Even in the midst of a blackout and battling a panic attack, I can still manage to be super awkward around Heath.

I should win some kind of award for this level of tenacity.

After trying and failing to regulate my breathing, I realize that part of the problem—aside from the fact that darkness is all around me and I'm living my worst nightmare, obviously—is that Heath's arm is still wrapped around my waist.

Which means I am incapable of taking a deep breath. Not that his grip is that tight, but because I am literally incapable of moving beneath his touch. His arm is hot and firm, and I don't have to see his arm to know just how muscular it is.

I am aware of Heath's toned arms. Good Lord, am I aware.

I suppose one doesn't become a first-string varsity basketball player without having fantastic arms. But right now, I could do without that knowledge.

I have to force my stomach muscles to expand so I can draw in a deep breath.

This means letting Heath in on the fact that I don't have a perfectly flat belly, but I'm well aware that staying conscious is far more important.

It still feels forced, though, when I draw in that first deep breath. When I exhale, I notice that Heath unclenches his death grip on me and while his arm is still there, it's not holding me down.

Is he scared too?

"You okay?" he asks. His voice is totally normal.

I nod again before once again remembering that he can't see me. "I'm okay."

And he's obviously *not* scared. I'm the only high school senior here who still uses a nightlight at home.

So wonderful. Great. Just when I'd thought this train ride couldn't be worse, my worst fears have now been outed to my crush.

Gah! My hands automatically grip his arm again as the train gives a little jerk.

Any calm I might have found thanks to my newfound ability to breathe flies out the window as my mind races with images that are too ridiculous to name.

There is no way Pennywise is on this train. I know this to be true. And yet all I can think of right now is the creepy clown from *IT* coming toward us.

The sound of a door being thrown open is quickly followed by the conductor's voice telling everyone to stay calm. The power will be up again shortly and they'll get us off this train.

"Get us off this train?" My voice is high and breathless.

Crap. I sound just like a girl in a horror movie.

The girl who's first to die because she panics and runs. Which I'm about to do. My whole body is tensed for flight, even though I can't make out an exit and wouldn't know how to pry open a door even if I found it.

Not to mention, Heath's now holding onto me as tightly as I'm holding onto him.

I tell myself he's scared too, but I know I'm lying.

"Breathe through a straw," I whisper. Not to Heath. To myself. But it's Heath who answers.

"You need a straw?" His low voice is edged with concern.

No doubt for my sanity.

I shut my eyes with a silent groan, and...it helps. I hold on to his arm a little tighter because I feel weirdly ungrounded sitting here with my eyes shut, but some of the fear eases.

I guess the reptile portion of my brain responsible for flight or fight can convince itself that this darkness isn't all around me. It's just that my eyes are closed.

Stupid amygdala.

But I'll take whatever relief I can find so I keep clutching Heath as I sit there with eyes clenched shut.

I realize that Heath's waiting for me to speak. He probably thinks I should explain the whole straw comment.

"Um..." I say. I have to stop to swallow because my mouth feels like I've taken a trek across the Sahara. I have no idea if that's because of the situation or the boy. Doesn't really matter, I guess. "Um, my yoga instructor says we should breathe in through our nose and then exhale through pursed lips like we're blowing out of a straw."

Yeah. Because that makes much more sense.

"When we're stressed," I tack on.

"Got it." I'm almost positive he thinks I'm insane, but he doesn't sound concerned anymore. If anything, I think I detect a hint of laughter there.

Not the mean kind. Heath Reilly is not a mean guy—though I've often wished he was. It would be so easy to get over this stupid, tongue-tying, heart-racing, palm-sweating crush if he would just be an a-hole now and again, you know?

But no. Mr. Broody McSexy has to be a good guy. A *nice* guy.

Way too nice for the likes of Pamela, if you ask me. But...you know. He's never asked me.

Something outside makes a high-pitched squeaking noise and it sets my pulse racing again. At this point, poor Heath's going to have scratch marks all over his arm.

But rather than pull away, my too-nice-for-life crush leans in closer and...snuggles?

That's the only term that applies to what he's doing. I stiffen as he shifts toward me and tugs me into his side so he's sorta spooning me from the side while sitting upright.

"You need to relax," he says. "You're shaking."

Am I? I hadn't even noticed, but now that he's mentioned it, I realize I am.

God, this could not be more embarrassing.

"Better?" he asks after he's situated his free arm around my shoulders and starts rubbing my arm.

I nod.

He's finagled it so my head is against his chest, which does nothing to help my racing heart, but that burst of awareness is leveled out by how soothing it is to feel the rumble of his voice when he speaks.

It's like catnip. I want to feel it again but I'm a little afraid that if I do I'll start purring and rubbing my head against his chest like a cat begging to be scratched.

So we stay like that in silence and listen to the chaos going on around us. A kid is crying. A man is on his phone yelling about the terrible state of public transportation in this country. A woman is barking orders to someone about the catered lunch meeting she's going to miss.

And we just sit there.

"So," he says after a while.

"So," I say while telling myself not to think about the fact that he's cuddling me.

"You ready for your presentation in New York?" he asks.

While this topic is not exactly relaxing, it's mundane enough that it actually does help me relax. "No," I say honestly. "I decided to do a solo presentation in addition to the group one and I don't have it memorized as well as I should."

He makes a noise of acknowledgement. Little more than a grunt but hearing that rumble in his chest is so weirdly satisfying that I feel even more of the tension ease.

I close my eyes again, and that helps too. Enough so that I'm able to loosen my grip on his arm. "Sorry about that," I murmur.

"No problem." He's so freakin' laid back.

Always has been.

As someone who's known him since he's five, I can say this with authority. Even in kindergarten he didn't yell or cry like the rest of us. He'd go with the flow, even then. He'd share his lunch with the kid who was crying over not having a dessert in their lunchbox. He'd include anyone who wanted to play during recess. He was quite possibly the only kid in the history of kids who didn't do temper tantrums and waterworks.

And now, at seventeen, he's the guy who cuddles the wackadoodle who's still afraid of the dark.

"What's your presentation on?" he asks.

I blink my eyes open and then immediately squeeze them shut again. For the life of me I can't tell if he's honestly interested, trying to keep me distracted, or just plain bored and hoping to be entertained.

"Um, it's a new business presentation, so I'm going to

pitch a startup idea." I take a deep breath, and when I continue, giving him way more info than he needs about my presentation, I realize that it's working.

Whether it was his intention or not, thinking about my presentation and talking about it... I'm distracted. My pulse starts to calm, which is a miracle, quite frankly, considering who I'm currently snuggling.

After a minute of talking and answering his questions about when I'd joined the club and why, I even risk opening my eyes.

And this time, I don't freak.

In fact, with Heath's low voice next to my ear drowning out the crazy going on around us, and with his whole body wrapped around me keeping me warm and grounded, I'm starting to feel almost...relaxed.

More relaxed, at least, than I typically am around Heath.

"What about you?" I ask when I tire of talking about my own involvement in the entrepreneurial club. It's not exactly an interesting story. I've always wanted to strike out on my own. My dad owns his own business—a successful one—and I always knew I'd do the same one day. Be my own boss. Chart my own course.

Sure, maybe I could do that working for a company, but I'd rather follow in my dad's footsteps and pursue my own goals. Not because I'm such a daddy's girl, but because I've seen the alternative. My mom gave up all her own dreams when she met my dad and now her life revolves around him like he's the center of the universe.

That's definitely not what I want for myself.

"What's your presentation about?" I prompt again because he still hasn't answered.

Heath shifts slightly beneath my cheek, the only indication that he's not entirely at ease with my question.

"Uh, I don't really have a presentation," he says.

I blink into space. "What do you mean? You're going to the conference, right?"

The presentations are the whole point of this trip.

"Yeah, but..." He exhales loudly. "I didn't really do anything for the joint presentation. I guess somebody dropped out...?" He paused and I nod as I put the pieces together. Peter Jenkins dropped out of Pamela's group project at the last minute. I'd heard they'd gotten someone to fill in, but I hadn't known who. I'd been too caught up in my last-minute project to give it much thought. But now, it's all so clear.

"So you're just here for Pamela." I hate that I said that aloud.

It's possible all this snuggling is making me *too* comfortable.

"Yeah, I guess you could say that," he says, his voice impossible to read.

I take a deep breath and inhale Heath's distinctive scent. The one I truly believe Downy should duplicate and manufacture because every woman in the world would happily bask in it. It's all soap and laundry detergent and...boy.

But in a good way. It's earthy and homey and makes me imagine what it would be like to be his girlfriend and wear his sweatshirts.

Is that too weird? Probably.

And this right here is why I avoid the guy like the plague.

Except for now. Because right now he is all that stands between me and Pennywise.

The thought makes me stiffen with another burst of fear, and Heath must notice because his arms tighten around me and he leans in and murmurs softly against my hair. "I've got you."

It's so freakin' sweet I think I might cry.

I don't, thank God. But the urge is there.

"Sorry, I just…I don't like the dark," I say.

He nods and once again his lips brush my hair. "Yeah. I got that."

There's only a hint of amusement in his voice, and it's not the mean kind, so I let out a huff of amusement as well. "I feel super lame right now," I admit.

"Hmm." He moves his head again and this time I wonder if he's doing the whole lip grazing thing on purpose. "*You* feel lame? I'm pretty sure I'm the one who just got dumped for all the world to hear."

I let out a little hiss as I wince. He gives this low, self-deprecating laugh in response. "I know you heard all that."

Maybe it's because I truly feel sorry for the guy, but I actually manage a joke. "Heard all what?"

He laughs again at my poorly feigned ignorance and this time it's less rueful and more genuine. Not surprisingly, Heath has a really great laugh.

Because of course he does.

Before I can say anything else, the conductor's voice fills the space, telling us we're going to evacuate in a calm, orderly fashion. He and another train employee have flashlights and they direct us into a line. It's only when Heath helps me up and into the aisle, his hands at my waist behind me, that I realize there are dim emergency lights lining the aisle.

I guess it hadn't been quite as dark as I'd thought. But

now we're about to head out into a pitch black tunnel so...not exactly making me feel any better right now.

"Heath?" I whisper.

Despite the cacophony going on as angry and emotional passengers make their feelings known as they line up behind us, Heath hears me. "I've got you, Celia." He slides one hand down and reaches for my hand.

The feel of his warm hand wrapping around me gives me a surge of courage—right before we dive into the darkness.

FOUR

Heath

IT IS SO black in this tunnel. So black. Like, blacker than black.

I'm not gonna lie. I'm a little creeped out about what might come scurrying out of the corners, and I'm not even afraid of the dark.

Celia grips my hand harder as I follow her down the last step, which is where the light from the flashlights ends and an incredibly dim, blink-and-you'd-miss-it strip of glow tape begins.

But we don't really need the tape because the far end of the tunnel glows with daylight.

If I thought the sight would make her less afraid, I'd have been wrong. Her grip grows tighter and I clench my teeth to keep from groaning.

For a girl so tiny, she has a grip of steel.

I reposition my free hand on her waist just to let her know I'm there. "Want me to go first?"

"No. I'm afraid of..." She doesn't finish as she glances behind her nervously. I don't push. Instead, I let her lead the way, and soon we're following behind the passengers in the train car ahead of us, and while the progress is slow and she never lets go of my hand, I swear I can feel her excitement as we draw closer to the light.

Once we're out, she draws in a deep breath and turns to me. She blinks as her eyes adjust to the light and then her gaze drops to our joined hands and...she blushes.

The girl *blushes*.

I don't think I've ever seen her blush before, but she's blushing now like she's never held a guy's hand before.

I feel a smile tugging at my lips because it's so freakin' cute.

But then she drops my hand like a hot potato and I'm reminded yet again that Celia Kennedy hates me.

And if she hadn't before, she did now. I'd heard the disdain clear as day in her voice. *So you're just here for Pamela?*

Crap. When she put it like that, I sounded pathetic. It had taken everything in me not to start spouting off excuses. Pamela had begged me to go. She'd done that pouting thing she always does, and had made all sorts of promises of the fun weekend we'd have together in the big city.

And like an idiot, I'd caved.

Celia's looking around us at the empty fields that line the tracks as more passengers spill out of the tunnel behind us.

"Should we...?" She gestures toward a spot where the others are starting to congregate on the grass.

"After you." I gesture toward the grass and she finds us a spot a little removed from the others. She's crossed her arms over her bag and is clutching it to her chest as we stand there. That's when I realize there's a chill in the air and the wind must be cutting straight through that short-sleeved blouse and little skirt she's wearing.

I tip my head down to hide another grin as I shrug out of my hooded sweatshirt.

Celia is the only girl I know who dresses so preppy. I'm not sure I've ever seen her in a jeans and T-shirt because she's always dressed like she's heading to the country club or a society luncheon.

Anyone else would look like a middle-aged accountant but she looks freakin' cute as a button in the pale pink blouse and tan, pleated skirt.

I hold the sweatshirt out to her, and for a minute she stares at it with a frown. "You'll be cold," she says.

I'm only wearing a T-shirt underneath, sure, but at least I've got jeans on. I realize she's not going to take it so I shift to wrap it around her shoulders. "You're cold *now*," I say by way of explanation.

She presses her lips together, her wide eyes absurdly large now as she assesses me like I'm some terrifying unknown.

I just barely hold back a sigh.

Seriously? She's still looking at me like I'm the big bad wolf even now after we'd...

Well, I wouldn't say we'd *bonded*, but we'd had a moment, right? Back there on the train, that was by far the most words she'd spoken to me since grade school.

I turn away to face the action, watching as the beleaguered train employees deal with a whole lot of cranky travelers.

"Another train is already on its way," a woman in

uniform is shouting. "Just stay calm and we'll have you and your luggage transferred over just as soon as we can."

Celia shifts from foot to foot beside me, and I see her knuckles are white where she's clutching her bag over her chest. Her poor satchel is taking the force of her death grip, I see.

"As soon as we can," she repeats with a furrowed brow. "I wonder how long that'll be."

I shake my head as I shrug. I can't even hazard a guess. I glance around us again and realize I don't even know where we are.

I mean, we couldn't have gone too far, right? But I don't see any landmarks or buildings in the distance to give me any perspective. "Maybe you should call someone for a ride," I say.

"Maybe." She nibbles on her lower lip as she thinks that over.

I've always known that Celia is a pretty girl. Not strikingly hot, or crazy sexy, but she's always been cute. But as she stands there stewing over her options, I find myself stewing over her.

I'm rarely this close to Celia, thanks to her aversion to me, but right now I'm free to study her and I realize she's not just cute. She's beautiful.

Sure, she's got a cute little button nose, but she also has high cheekbones and a heart-shaped face. And her mouth...

Her mouth is this perfect little bow. Even her eyebrows are somehow...dainty.

And no, I've never used the word *dainty* to describe anything before in my life. But it fits her to a tee. She's adorable and elegant all at once. Like a doll, but the old-fashioned kind made out of porcelain that no one's ever allowed to touch.

Certainly not a guy like me. She's always made that perfectly clear.

Not that she's a snob, or anything. She's too sweet to be a snob. But I do think she knows her own worth. And when she looks at me?

Well, I'm pretty sure she sees exactly what I'm worth too.

She's never bought this lie that I'm cool. And she's always made it clear she doesn't buy the hype and she isn't about to overpay for a knockoff.

Not that she'd ever say that, of course. Again…too nice.

She turns to face me fully with a frown. "Even if I can get someone to pick us up, we need to get to Elmdale to get the next train," she says. "I don't know how far that is. Do you?"

I stare at her in silence because…she can't be serious. But she's already got her phone in hand and is muttering something about looking up how long the drive is.

"Or," I say. "We could just tell Mr. Deckman that our train derailed and go back home."

I arch my brows. Because that would be the *sane* thing to do, no?

Her widened eyes tell me this is the wrong response. "No," she says. "No way."

She shakes her head for emphasis and long dark locks go flying. The breeze helps and soon she's dropping her satchel to swat hair out of her face.

I go to help and find myself running my fingers down the side of her face in an attempt to push her hair out of the way. It's a weirdly intimate touch, and—

And now she's staring up at me like I'm Frankenstein's monster.

So, that's cool.

I drop my hands, suddenly feeling like some perv for touching her.

Irritation flares and I turn to face the train. I swear I'm not a cocky dude, but...have I mentioned that most girls like me?

I mean, I'm not a *bad* guy.

I'm not a saint either, obviously, and I definitely don't buy into my own hype. But I'm not some sketchy loser either.

She exhales loudly. "Sorry, it's just..."

I turn to face her and she's biting her lip again.

"What is it?" It's possible my voice isn't as frustration-free as I'd intended.

She flinches in response. "I can't miss this presentation," she blurts out, her voice louder than I'd ever heard it. "I really can't."

Her eyes go wide and pleading, and my irritation fades.

Ah crap. Her wide-eyed puppy dog look might be even worse than Pamela's pouting. No, it's definitely more effective because there's absolutely nothing disingenuous about this look whereas everything Pamela does has a hidden purpose. She's manipulative and I know it. I've always known it.

So why do I keep taking her back?

I sigh. That's the question of the day, I guess.

Celia keeps talking, all about how some dean is going to be there and how this is her big chance, and—

Holy crap. Celia Kennedy is talking to me.

I'm listening, I swear, but there's a big part of my brain that can only focus on how nice it is to have her looking at me like I'm a normal human being and not the big baddie straight out of her worst nightmares. And it's really nice to hear her opening up to me like I'm—well, like a friend.

I glance around at the strangers milling around us.

I guess I am the closest thing to a friend she has here.

On a rush of air, she hurries on. "But I totally understand if you want to bail. I mean, you're only in it for the trip to the city and...and your...your...Pamela."

We both flinch as she stumbles over those words. She'd been going to say *your girlfriend* and caught herself in time, but just barely.

I run a hand through my hair and look around again. I'm not sure whether to laugh or shout with frustration. She might understand that I want to bail, but she's not going to no matter how crazy this trek might be.

We both return to silence for a while, our gazes fixed down the tracks like a train's going to magically appear any second now. The longer we stand there not talking, the more her last words seem to eat away at me. *You're only in it for your Pamela*.

As if I wasn't feeling low enough after Pamela's latest I-can't-do-this speech, I now find myself squirming with frustration that this girl who never even deigns to speak to me thinks she knows my life.

"Pamela can be persuasive." I regret the words instantly.

Celia's brows arch slightly as she looks over at me. "I'm sure."

I can't tell if she's being sarcastic or not, and that's only more irritating. It would be one thing if she were to mock me outright, but it's like she's too nice to be truly mean.

Maybe I've spent too much time with Pamela, but I don't know how to deal with too nice.

"She made it seem like you guys needed someone to fill the spot," I continue.

A flash of something I can't name crosses Celia's eyes. "That's true," she says slowly, like she's afraid she's admitting too much. "We were looking for people. We'd signed up for a certain amount of slots and would have lost money, and maybe even been disqualified for some of the categories."

I nod as if I knew that. I didn't, but Pamela *had* used that argument to convince me.

Well, that and the promise of a romantic weekend away together to try and save our relationship.

Because even when we were fine, Pamela and I were never good. We had moments when Pamela was happy, and times when we got along without fighting, but there were never any times where we were truly happy.

But Pamela was the one who seemed to believe that we could be happy if we just worked for it. If *I* worked for it.

This weekend was supposed to be our opportunity to give *us* a fighting chance.

Those were *her* words. That was *her* argument. As of last week she'd wanted to fight for us, but apparently something or some*one* changed her mind.

The thought has me swallowing a wave of revulsion. She's cheated on me before. I knew it. She knew that I knew. But I'd thought we'd gotten past all that.

"I'm sorry," Celia says. It's so soft, I almost miss it.

When I glance over, she's looking down at the ground. "I'm sorry she...did that."

I take a deep breath and shrug even though she's not looking. "It's not exactly a surprise, I guess."

She gives a little huff of amusement and I do too. That's an understatement. There are a whole lot of running jokes among our friends about how toxic Pamela and I are for each other. We both know it, too, that's the sick thing.

But we're each other's worst bad habit, and bad habits are hard to kick.

I rub the back of my neck as I go back to watching for this highly anticipated next train.

This on-and-off again relationship isn't easy for me to talk about with my closest friends, but having Celia say she's sorry for me? My insides twist with humiliation.

I have no idea at what point I'd become such a cliche, but I want out. For real, this time.

"It would be a shame if you don't go," Celia says quietly.

I turn and stare down at the top of her head, certain I'd heard her wrong. And then it clicks. "Wait, will you guys get in trouble if I don't show?"

She shakes her head. "No. I don't think so. I mean..." She shrugs. "Maybe. But that's not what I meant. I just meant that this is a really good opportunity. It looks great on college applications, and Elijah and Noelle and some of our other friends are going to be there, and..." Her tongue flicks out to wet her lips and she takes a deep breath. "I just think it would be a shame, that's all. If you let Pamela take that away."

I stare at her for so long that she starts to blush again, but even then I can't bring myself to look away. "You think I'm pathetic, don't you?"

She glances up with wide eyes, her lips parted. "What? No! I never said that."

Said so sweetly it's all I can do not to laugh aloud at her obvious horror.

"No, you would never say that," I agree.

I'm ready to let it drop but she shifts toward me and starts fidgeting with her phone. "Look, I'm really not in a position to judge. I've never been in a relationship and I don't plan on being in one anytime soon. Not until college, at least," she says.

Her look of resolve is so strong it makes me wonder...

Twenty questions pop into my head at once, but mostly I'm dying to know why she's so anti-dating. What does she have against relationships? But then I'm sidetracked by another realization.

She really hasn't dated anyone.

I find myself gaping at her. I never thought about it much, but it's true. I've never once heard about Celia hooking up with a guy. Never heard about her being into anyone or being linked with someone.

My gaze drops to her lips. Has she ever been kissed?

My gut goes tight and hot as my mind imagines what it would be like to kiss her before I can stop myself.

"Anyway…" She drops her head, seemingly unaware that I've just envisioned making out with her and am now crazy turned on.

Crap.

"I shouldn't judge. I hear love makes everyone do stupid things." She tempers this with a sweet smile that tugs at my chest.

Love. Is that what I had with Pamela?

My gut says no.

My heart says definitely not.

But I don't say anything because Celia's suddenly all business. "I'll see if Ryan and Mara are still around," she says. "I'm sure they'd come and give you a lift home."

Give *me* a lift. Not her. Because this adorable little crazyface here is hellbent on getting to New York.

"Celia," I interrupt, just as she's pulling out her phone.

"Yes?" She blinks up at me, her hand still holding the phone in mid-air between us.

I sigh. "Let's take a moment to recap, shall we?"

Her lips twitch with amusement at that, and she drops the hand with the phone. "Okay."

I tick items off on my fingers. "We're in the middle of who-knows-where."

"Correct."

"Even if we get to Elmdale, we'd have to get there in time to make the connection."

She nods.

"And if we miss the connection?" I arch my brows, and Celia inexplicably responds with an optimistic smile.

"We won't." She scrambles to pull out the schedule and unfold it. She edges closer to me and I lean in, careful not to touch her lest she scream in horror. "See?" She points to fine-print gibberish. "As long as we make it there by 7, we'll catch the train."

I turn to face her and my immediate protest lodges in my throat in the face of her eager expression. She so wants me to say this is a good plan.

It's not. She has to see all the ways this could fail. But she's clearly desperate to make it to the city.

"Tell you what," I finally say, reaching for the phone she's holding out. "Let's try to find someone to pick us up and give us a ride to Elmdale to catch the train so we're not waiting out here in the cold for hours."

Her brows draw together and a little crease of concern forms above her nose.

I hurry to add, "And if we can't get a ride, we'll wait."

"Oh no," she shakes her head quickly. "You don't have to wait. If you can't get a ride home, we'll call you a taxi or something."

I stare at her in disbelief. "Celia."

"Yes?"

"Do you really think I'm going to leave you here, cold and alone and surrounded by strangers in the middle of nowhere?"

She blinks once. Twice. Guilt flickers in her eyes.

Yes, that guilt tells me. That's exactly what she thought.

I sigh as I snag her phone. "All right, let's start with our parents."

FIVE

Celia

AN HOUR PASSES, and I feel confident that I can speak for both of us when I say that we are miserable.

The wind is getting worse, and we're huddled together now because they won't let us on to get our carry-on luggage. The other passengers—those who haven't arranged to be picked up by car—are all as miserable as we are.

"Here." I thrust a granola bar at Heath and he shakes his head.

"I have two," I say, offering the second up for proof.

This is one thing I have learned about Heath today. Not only is he a nice guy, he's an obnoxiously noble one to boot.

It took nearly twenty minutes of nagging before he finally relented to sharing the sweatshirt.

Which means that we are back to cuddling. In a totally weird and platonic way, of course. I'm literally pressed against his side so we can both be zipped inside the hoodie.

"What about Addie?" he asks.

I wince at the obvious desperation in his voice. We're grasping at straws now because we've gone through every option at least twice. "I told you, she's visiting her dad's family this weekend. Remember?"

His hopeful expression falls flat and he goes back to glaring at the train tracks. When he opens his granola bar, I have to shift to accommodate the move. Not an easy feat since I'm currently tucked against his chest like I'm a freakin' baby kangaroo.

As much as I'm cold and anxious about making it to Elmdale and then onto New York, I feel even worse about Heath. It's my fault he's still here.

Well, it's my fault plus whatever bad juju has befallen us both today.

We've tried everyone in my phone at this point, not to mention Heath's dad. He couldn't remember his mom's number, and his phone won't turn on. So we're stuck with my contacts, and at this point I'm only turning my phone on occasionally to spare the battery because if we're both stuck out here without a phone, and in the middle of nowhere...

I shiver at the thought of how lost I'd feel. Heath wraps his arm around me tighter. "This is insane," he says. "How is no one picking up?"

I wince again. I've tried my parents twice but, just like this morning, they're MIA.

Same with Mara and Ryan. I can't blame them. When they didn't hear from me right away, they must have assumed I was on the train and well on my way. How could they possibly have anticipated a train derailment in the middle of nowhere?

Since they're together, I'm guessing they're studying, or watching a movie, or doing some stupid task for the senior scavenger hunt our friend Elijah planned. It's supposed to be just for fun, but Mara and Ryan are too competitive to do anything *just for fun*. So, yeah. They're probably off collecting lawn ornaments or something, blissfully unaware that their respective best friends are stranded.

And considering most of our other friends are currently en route to New York on the train we missed...

We're out of luck.

Again.

"I think maybe I'm cursed," I say.

He rubs my arm and back to help warm me up, his granola bar already devoured and the wrapper stashed in his back pocket.

I'm saving mine. I'm hungry but I don't think I can eat just yet. Between being anxious about arriving in New York on time, worrying about my still-unprepared presentation, and the constant state of alarm my body's been in thanks to Heath's presence, I'm a mess inside.

I'm like a snowglobe. Just when I think things have settled and maybe I can relax, something happens to turn me upside down and my insides are tossed around in a jumbled flurry.

"I should never have said yes to this trip," Heath says with a sigh.

I glance up at him and my heart gives a leap. From this point of view, I see his chiseled jaw, the start of some stubble, and his lips, which are curved down in a frown.

Guilt sucks. And this is definitely my fault. Oh, maybe not the derailment, but the fact that he's still here is all on me. I sigh as I pull back to bring my phone up between us, which stretches the sweatshirt fabric tight across my back.

I'm gonna owe him a new sweatshirt after this because there's no way it'll fit him properly after this.

"What are you doing?" he asks.

"I have my mom's credit card," I say. "I'm calling a car service."

I can feel his eyes on me. "Yeah?"

I nod, already typing in the name of a local taxi company, pretending I can't feel his stare on me and that it's not making my skin prickle and heat.

"Wait a second." He puts a hand over mine, covering the phone so I'm forced to look up.

His furrowed brows have drawn down now, and he's gone from his regularly brooding self to a way more dramatic brooding. He's basically Heathcliff on the moors.

He leans his head down a bit and the rest of the world ceases to exist because…oh my God. Heath's lips are so close I'd be kissing him if I went up on tiptoe.

I close my eyes and swallow hard.

Do not think about kissing Heath Reilly.

Man, this crush is annoying.

"Celia," he says quietly, an ominous tone in his voice.

"Yes?"

"Who are you calling the car for?" he asks.

"Um…" I look down at the phone in my hand, but his hand is covering mine so I end up ogling Heath's hand.

He has a really nice hand. Big, strong, manly.

Can hands be manly?

"Celia?" There's a definite warning in his tone, like he's getting ready to give me a lecture.

"It's for you," I say.

I set my shoulders as he lets out a huff. "Celia, I told you I'm not leaving you here."

"But this is silly," I say. "You shouldn't be freezing your butt off out here in the cold with me when you don't even want to go—"

His finger over my lips cuts me off.

I blink in surprise, my lips still parted. Holy crap. Heath Reilly is touching my lips.

"I'm not having this argument with you again," he says in that annoyingly calm tone of his. "I'm not leaving you here alone. That's final."

He's gazing down at me with such a serious look.

He wants to go home. Of course he does. Why wouldn't he? He's having an even worse day than I am, and he clearly doesn't care about the presentations or even seeing the city.

But I am not about to give up on the best chance I have of impressing the dean of the college I want to go to just because the guy I like has discovered chivalry.

I tug my head back and his finger drops. "Fine," I say, my tone short. "But I'm not leaving."

His brows draw down even further into a glower. "Then neither am I."

"Fine."

"Fine."

We're glaring at each other now, and it's getting super awkward. Mainly because we're pressed together from chest to toe.

Sort of hard to keep up a good angry glare while cuddling.

He seems to be thinking the same thing because he looks away first with a huff. "Look, I know this competition means a lot to you," he says.

I nod, looking straight ahead, which is a mistake because now all I'm aware of are his chest muscles. Guess who also has amazing pecs?

So unfair. Why does he have to be hot and nice and smart and funny and now a freakin' knight in shining armor?

How is a girl ever supposed to get over a crush on a guy like this?

He'd trailed off talking but I brace myself for the lecture to come. There's no doubt in my mind he's going to try to talk me into walking away from this trip.

He shifts, his arms tightening around me. "I'll make sure you get there."

My head snaps up and my eyes widen. That's so not where I thought he was going.

His lips quirk up in amusement. "You don't have to look so surprised."

I blink. Because I *am* surprised. "Thanks," I say. And then inspiration strikes. "I can still call the car company..."

He starts to frown but I shake my head. "No, I mean, I can call and see how much it would be to drive us to Elmdale."

His brows arch and before he says anything I have my phone in hand and am calling the car company. I flinch at the price of picking us up, but it's our best chance of making the train to New York so I get out the credit card and make the arrangements.

"They'll be here in thirty minutes," I say, relief flooding through me.

He grins down at me and...whoa.

Wow.

Brooding Heath is hot, but smiling Heath?

I look away because I'm positive he can feel my racing heart. How could he not with the way we're plastered together?

"Okay," he says, his tone lighter as he shifts his grip on me, finding a new comfortable way for us to huddle together. "Thirty minutes. We can do that."

I nod, but even as I do, the next thirty minutes seem to stretch out ahead of us like eternity.

"I know," he says suddenly. "Why don't you practice your presentation?"

I stare up at him. "Seriously?"

He nods, an adorable little smile still playing at his lips, his hazel eyes so warm and sweet, they make my heart do a backflip. "You said you were worried because you haven't practiced enough, right?"

I nod, just a little surprised that he remembered that.

At what point will I just accept the fact that he's too good to be true?

"Um, if you don't mind..." I start hesitantly.

He smirks and casts a meaningful look around us at our barren surroundings. The only sounds are coming from the remaining passengers, talking amongst themselves. "I think I can make time in my busy schedule."

I laugh and reach into my bag to fish out my notecards. "Okay, if you're sure."

He holds a hand out. "It'll give me something to do."

I hand over the cards, flutter my hands like an idiot before settling them on his chest, and then I find a place on the collar of his T-shirt to focus my gaze as I launch into my presentation.

A little while later, he's no doubt bored to tears as I come to the end.

"Nice work," he says with a smile that's filled with so much pride, I feel it deep down in my chest.

"Thanks." I go to take the cards, but he holds onto them. "You just missed this one section here." He points to the card and I groan, forgetting myself for a moment and letting my head fall against his chest.

His chuckle sounds delicious when I'm this close.

I pull away quickly, and heat creeps into my cheeks at having laid my head against his chest. I hope like heck he doesn't think I'm trying to take advantage of the situation.

He doesn't seem to care though, because when I glance up he's still smiling down at me. "What's the matter?"

"That section on sustainability is the most important part," I explain. "It's what makes my idea so different from how these businesses are normally run." I shake my head as I read over the section I forgot. "I can't believe I left this out."

"We'll just have to practice some more," he says.

I nod, not trusting myself to speak. *We'll* just have to practice?

My heart trips and falls. A girl could get used to being part of a *we* like that.

The thought has alarm bells ringing and I back up a step, then two, breaking the cozy warmth of our makeshift little cocoon as I stand apart from him.

This is why it's dangerous to get close to Heath Reilly. One afternoon together and I'm already forgetting that I don't want a relationship.

If he actually liked me back?

If he kissed me and smiled at me like this all the time?

I gulp down air as I turn my head away. The thought makes me feel even more lost than not having my phone while stranded in the middle of nowhere.

My stomach sinks and my head reels.

Not good.

This is so not good. I need to get away from this guy before I fall any further. Before I fall so far I forget who I am and what I want.

I push away from his chest as far as the sweatshirt allows. Oh crap, I'm trapped. A wave of panic has me reaching for the zipper. I'll risk the cold for some much needed space.

Heath's frowning at me in confusion, but I glance around and see the people who are remaining. "I'm gonna go see if anyone wants to share a car with us. We can't be the only ones running out of time and patience."

"Good thinking," he says. "Why don't I go see about our bags again?"

I nod. "Good idea."

Last time we'd asked, we'd been snapped at by the surly conductor. So far everyone that's gone has left without their luggage, but it couldn't hurt to try.

We each go our own ways, and the cold air and distance from Heath's intoxicating presence helps to clear my head. A little while later when the car arrives, we're back together —still without luggage, sadly, but with an older couple who've offered to give us cash to pay for their half of the ride to Elmdale.

Heath said the railroad employees won't let anyone on board because of safety issues but that they'll get our luggage to us. They gave him a number to call, but I still want to cry at the thought of showing up at our hotel in New York with only the clothes on my back.

Noelle's my roommate, though. If anyone has clothes to spare, it'll be her.

They won't fit, obviously. She's way taller and has the kind of curves I can only dream of, but at least they'll be clean.

I shiver.

They'll be clean and *warm*.

God, I hope she has lots of sweaters. I'm so chilled to the bone, I feel like I'll never get warm again. I tug Heath's sweatshirt tighter around me—he insisted it was my turn to wear it when he caught me shivering.

He holds the car door open for the older couple to slide into the backseat.

There's only two seats in the back, with a divider armrest in the middle, and so it's instantly clear where Heath and I will be stuck for the long drive to Elmdale.

He gives me a sympathetic wince and a rueful smile as he gets in and gestures to his lap. "At least we'll be warm?" he offers.

I let out a rueful huff of laughter and climb in with a resigned sigh.

I settle in on Heath's admittedly comfortable lap and after a second of hesitation, his arms close around me.

Once again, we're cuddling.

I sigh as I rest my head against his shoulder and feel his lips graze the top of my head.

I'm starting to get used to being near Heath, and that's terrifying.

And amazing.

His arm strokes my arm as if out of habit. I guess he's gotten used to this too.

Being this close to him is still weird. It's still Heath, the guy I've been avoiding for years. But it's not painfully awkward, and it's not tense.

It's comfortable and uncomfortable all at once.

But mostly it's just confusing.

SIX

Heath

I'M CONFUSED as hell by the way I respond to Celia.

She's female, yes. But this is hardly the first time I've been close to a girl. I shouldn't be this hyper aware of her scent, the warmth of her skin, the texture of her hair when it brushes my cheek...

All of it. I am excruciatingly aware of all of it, and I have been ever since I sat next to her on that train.

So yeah. It's confusing.

But I'm even more confused by the way she acts around me. And I don't mean physically. She's clearly getting more comfortable around me in that sense—a full day spent spooning and snuggling and cuddling will likely have that effect. So it's not just that.

It's the way she looks at me now. Like, she's still scared of me, but...it's different.

Or, it's the same but I'm seeing more because she can't turn and run away from me like she normally would. So now I see that fear there when she looks at me—but I don't think she's actually scared of *me*.

No one would fret over the person who scares them, and she won't stop worrying about me and my comfort. If it were up to her, I'd be safe at home and tucked in bed with a cup of cocoa right now and not traveling even further from Lakeview in the hopes that we'll make another train that will hopefully get us into the city sometime in this lifetime.

She climbs out of the car first when we arrive in Elmdale and I follow more slowly. I need at least a solid minute of non-touching time to try and get my head on straight.

As is, my heart is pounding, my blood is boiling with desire, and my head is spinning as I try to make sense of her every glance, every comment, every expression.

No matter how much I try to figure her out, though, it doesn't add up.

I can't reconcile the determined, confident, kind, thoughtful girl I've been getting to know today with the scared, standoffish, disdainful chick who's been ignoring me for roughly a decade.

It doesn't make sense.

And being forced to hold her on my lap and remind myself over and over again that we're just friends—if that—for the duration of the drive is not helping anything.

We get to the Elmdale train station just in time for the nice older couple to catch their train bound for Boston, and then Celia and I are on our own.

Again.

The train station is an open situation, and there's a bunch of automated stations but not many people around. We find the right track and a bus shelter type structure to huddle in.

"At least we're protected from the wind," she says with a hopeful look that makes my chest grow tight.

"True luxury right here," I say. I'm obviously being sarcastic but I try to soften it with a smile.

She dips her head with a little laugh. "Thanks for coming with me all this way," she says as she pulls out that cursed schedule.

"What are you looking up now?" I ask.

She's nibbling on her lower lip and I have to tear my gaze away because staring at her lips is not helping this new painful awareness situation I've got going on.

"I'm checking to see when there's a train back to Lakeview," she says.

For me.

Because she's still more worried about getting me home then she is about taking a night train into the city and arriving in Manhattan close to midnight.

A long silence passes as she tries to make sense of that chart and I find myself debating whether she's so intent on sending me home because she wants to get rid of me or because she feels sorry for me.

Neither of those options makes me feel great.

I mean, sure, there's a possibility that she's just looking out for my best interests, but odds are she's trying to spare me the agony of being at the same hotel with my ex on the trip that was supposed to be our romantic weekend away together.

But I can't stop thinking about something she'd said earlier. About how it would be a shame if I let Pamela keep me from having a weekend in a new city with my friends.

I glance over at Celia.

Are we friends now?

Maybe.

Maybe not.

I have no idea how she'll act around me when we're no longer stuck together like this. She could very well go back to pretending I don't exist.

Which is fine, obviously.

It doesn't matter to me.

Celia sets down the schedule and takes out her phone. "I should let Noelle know the new plan so she and Mr. Deckman don't worry." She presses her lips together as she studies me. "Do you want me to tell them you'll be there tonight too or should I tell them you can't make it?"

Decision time. Her gaze meets mine and there's a kindness there that slays me. This is a rare sight…for me, at least. She's looking at me with this openness that I never see from her.

And she's worried. About me. And all at once, I see my situation from her point of view.

Did Pamela hurt me so badly that I can't face her?

Will I waste my time and money that I already spent on this trip and turn back to sulk at home?

"Tell them I'm coming," I say. "Why not?" I glance around at the deserted station. "I've already come this far, right?"

She gives me a half smile that I can't interpret. "Okay. If you're sure."

She's definitely not jumping for joy, but it wasn't like I was expecting her to.

"I'm sure." I lean back against the plastic shelter. "It might be fun to check out New York."

"You've never been?" She's turning on her cell and gives me a curious glance.

"Never. You?"

She shakes her head, and there's a pink tinge to her

cheeks, but this time it's a flush of excitement. "I've always wanted to go. There are so many things I want to do during our off time." She flinches as she glances at her satchel where the notecards are held. "After the hard part's behind me."

"Like what?" I ask as she types out a text to Noelle.

"Central Park, The Met, Broadway..." She glances over with a grin that makes my heart stop.

Like, it stopped so abruptly I may have died for a second.

I've seen this smile on her tons of times, but never aimed at me.

Never *for* me.

"I'm guessing there won't be time to do it all in one weekend, but I'm going to try," she finishes before turning her attention back to her phone.

"Look out New York, Celia's coming for you," I say in a bland tone that makes her laugh.

Her laugh stops short, though, and her smile fades, along with any pink in her cheeks.

She's gone deathly pale beside me at whatever texts Noelle is sending her. At least, I assume it's Noelle responding to her texts.

"Everything okay?" I ask. "You're not kicked out of the competition because you're running a little late, right?"

I meant it to be a joke, but by the pained look on her face, I'm a little worried that's exactly what happened.

Crap.

"Look, Celia, we'll talk to Mr. Deckman first thing—"

"No, that's...that's not it," she says. When she looks over at me, I see it—*pity*.

Oh hell.

"What is it?" I ask.

"I don't believe in spreading gossip," she says, which she follows up with a pursed lip look of determination that would be funny if dread wasn't pooling in my gut.

I stick my hand out. "Give me the phone, Celia."

She winces and hesitates, but a second later she hands it over and Noelle's text is glaring up at me from the screen.

Noelle: I'm glad you're not alone, but you might want to give Heath a heads up before he gets here. Pamela's telling anyone who will listen about how she's with Dominic now.

My mouth goes dry but I can't bring myself to look away.

Dominic. I have a hazy image in my head. He's new. He and his twin sister Jazmin joined our class at the start of the school year. But that wasn't even two weeks ago, so while I know that he's supposed to be some amazing basketball player and he'll be joining our team, I haven't spent any time with him.

I think I said hi to him once when he sat with me and some of the other guys from the team at lunch, but that's about it.

But apparently Pamela's been spending time with him.

That dread turns to lead in my stomach and the taste of bile fills my throat.

She'd cheated on me. If they're together then that's what that means.

I shouldn't be surprised.

Hell, I'm not surprised. I'm feeling a whole slew of emotions right now but surprise isn't one of them. Mainly I just feel disgust. With her, yes...but also with myself.

How was I here? *Again?*

"I'm sorry, Heath," Celia murmurs at my side.

I nod, but I don't drag my eyes away from that text.

Which is how I'm the first to see Noelle's next text when it pops up on the screen.

Noelle: You must be in hell right now. Stuck with Heath, of all people? Dude, that sucks. Hang in there, girl. Can't wait til you get here!

I frown down at the text just as Celia snatches the phone from my hand and hugs it to her chest.

Stuck with Heath?

I stare at Celia hard, like if I look long enough and with the right amount of intensity I might be able to get what's going on there.

Because the thing is, Noelle and I are friends. She hangs out with me, Ryan, Elijah, and the other guys all the time. I know she's not saying it sucks because *she* thinks I'm so horrible.

She's saying it sucks because *Celia* thinks I'm so horrible.

As I stare at Celia and she blushes and looks away—I feel it. The betrayal I should be feeling over Pamela cheating on me is there, but it's over Celia.

I feel freakin' betrayed by Celia.

How dumb is that?

I know it makes no sense to feel this way, but I've never been anything but nice to her. Did I insult her at some point? Did I accidentally run over her pet and no one told me?

I scrub a hand over my face and turn away, more frustrated now than when Pamela stood me up and dumped me in public.

I don't really do anger. I'm not good at it. Everyone jokes about how I brood and angst, or whatever, and maybe there's some truth to that. My relationship with Pamela has given me a lot to brood about.

But I never really get angry with her. Not even today with this latest crap she pulled. Some part of me always expects this from her.

You can't get hurt when you see it coming from a mile away, right?

But Celia...

Much as I've always thought she didn't like me, I guess I always kinda hoped there was some other explanation.

But no. She definitely hates me. So...awesome. No wonder she's been so hellbent on sending me home.

"Are you okay?" Her soft voice next to me makes me start.

"Yeah. Fine."

She nods and kicks her feet that dangle a little above the ground because she's so short. For the first time since before the train derailed, we're stuck in awkward silence.

No, not just awkward. It's painful, tense, *brutal* silence.

And this time I'm not gonna be the one to break it.

The ringing of her phone makes us both sit up with a start and she scrambles to answer it. Her phone's not broken, but like with my call with Pamela earlier, I can hear her mom's loud voice from where I'm sitting.

"Cece," she says, her tone plaintive and high. "What's going on? I got your messages and we're worried."

"You okay, Peanut?" A male voice chimes in. Clearly they have her on speaker and it sounds like they're driving.

Celia tips her head down and with her free hand grips the bench so hard her knuckles turned white. "Mom, you took my car without asking."

"Well, honey, your dad had a meeting in Boston and he wanted me to join him."

"You're in...you're in Boston?" she asks.

"You were going away this weekend, weren't you? Or

you're staying with a friend..." Her mom's tone is one of someone taking a stab in the dark and hoping she hits the bullseye.

"Yeah, something like that," Celia says.

Her voice is perfectly even. I'm the only one who can see how hard she's clutching the bench and that her jaw is clenched so tight, I'm starting to worry she's going to cry.

They talk for a little while longer and it's clear that they don't know where she's heading or why, let alone that she's been stranded with a guy she hates in a town she doesn't know on the way to the most important event of her life.

Just like that, my anger fades. It's replaced by a sympathy that makes my chest burn. I want to wrap an arm around her again and tug her close. Not for warmth but because she's hurting.

She hides it well, but it's obvious to me as she says her goodbyes and tells them she'll see them next week.

She doesn't say anything and we go back to staring at the empty tracks.

I look at the hanging clock and realize it's getting close to seven. Shouldn't there be other people around?

I know I'd said I wasn't going to break the silence, but that was before, and now she's sitting next to me, kicking her legs like a little kid and looking more abandoned than I can handle.

"So," I say.

She glances over with a small smile that hides nothing. "So."

I feign an avid interest in the tracks ahead of us. "Cece, huh?"

She lets out a choked laugh. "No one calls me that but my mom."

"I don't know," I tease. "I like it. Cece. It's cute."

I glance over in time to catch her nose crinkling up in disgust.

"What?"

"I hate being called cute. It's what people always call short girls who aren't smokin' hot."

"You can be hot and cute," I correct her, donning an authoritative voice to hide the fact that I'm basically admitting aloud that I think she's hot.

"Uh huh." She sounds unconvinced.

"So no Cece then," I say with a sigh. I pause before adding, "I guess you prefer Peanut."

Her laugh is so stinkin' adorable, but I can't tell her that because I'd be willing to bet she's not fond of being called adorable either.

Which is a shame, because she is adorable. And cute.

And yeah, she's also smokin' hot.

"Only my dad calls me that," she says through her laughter.

"Fine, fine." I pretend to be disappointed, and can't stop a stupid grin because I cheered her up, at least a little.

But she still hates you, dumbass.

I shove aside the thought. I have to believe I've made some progress today.

"You two kids need to git," an old guy with a Southern drawl calls from the far end of the platform.

Celia and I share a shocked stare before turning back to find him making a shooing motion with his hands. "Go on, now," he says. "There's no loitering here."

"But..." Celia looks at me in clear confusion.

"We're waiting for our train," I say to the stranger.

He stalks toward us with a frown. "There ain't no more trains coming through here, not in either direction."

"Are you sure?" Celia asks, her voice high. She whips out her schedule and holds it out for him as proof.

His frown intensifies as he glances at it and back to her. "Where'd you get that? That's the old schedule. They changed the times last month. That's old information."

Her lips part and for the first time all day I see her eyes glimmer with tears.

"Thank you, sir," I say, taking over because Celia looks like she's stunned speechless.

"Sorry y'all got stuck, but you can't stay here," he says with one last parting glare before he walks away.

When I turn to Celia, she's staring up at me with wide, tear-filled eyes, and I kid you not, her lower lip is quivering.

I thought that was only something that happened in cartoons, but this girl has the whole quivering lip thing in spades and it just about breaks my heart in two.

"This is the worst day," she whispers in a tight, teary voice.

I don't think before reaching for her and tugging her close for a hug. She burrows into my chest with a sniff and lets me hug her for a long while.

"We'll figure this out," I say. "Your solo presentation isn't until tomorrow afternoon, right?"

She nods. "The group ones are in the morning, but—"

"If you don't show for those, they'll be fine without you," I assure her. "What matters is that we get you there for the solo presentation, and assuming we can get a train in the morning, we can still make it."

She sniffs and nods against my chest, her fingers curling into the material of my T-shirt. "Okay," she says with another nod. "Okay, we can make it."

I smile as I dip my head and press my lips to the top of

her head. She might hate me, but I can't bring myself to feel the same.

I like this girl. A lot.

And I'm going to get her to that presentation if it's the last thing I do.

SEVEN

Celia

I AM A COMPETENT WOMAN. I don't need a guy to help me.

This is what I tell myself as I haul my hand cart full of supplies through the fluorescent-lit aisles of the twenty-four hour drugstore we found near the station. Around the corner is the motel where Heath booked us a room with my mom's credit card.

While I'm grateful that he stepped in and took charge, I'm still trying to convince myself that I would have been just fine without him. Yes, I'm exhausted and emotionally spent, and being alone in a strange place would have been scary. But I would have found that motel on my own. And I would have found a place to score food eventually, too.

So, no, I don't *need* Heath to help me. I snag some face wash and throw it in my cart with a sigh. But I can also admit that he's been a huge help and I'm grateful he's here.

I should probably tell him that.

I cringe at the memory of Noelle's text. *Stuck with Heath, of all people? Dude, that sucks.*

Had he seen it?

I still don't know.

I'd grabbed the phone quickly, and he'd clearly been distracted by the news about Pamela and Dominic.

Is it too much to ask that he hadn't read it?

Maybe.

I shift my hand cart from one hand to the other. It's starting to get heavy with all the essentials I'm gathering for my night in a motel room. With Heath Reilly.

Alone. In a motel room. With Heath Reilly.

I blow air out through an imaginary straw as I scan this aisle for a toothbrush and toothpaste. Heath's on the other side of the store stocking up on enough snacks and junk food to hopefully equal a meal. We couldn't find any restaurants nearby that were still open so we're making do with what we've got.

"You ready?" he asks as he turns into my aisle, his own hand cart overflowing with what looks to be a whole lot of chips and an alarming amount of beef jerky.

"Yup." I nod toward the back section. "I found some clothes back there if you want something to change into." I grin as I hold up an ugly, bright purple sweatshirt with a rainbow and a unicorn emblazoned on the front. "They might have one in your size too."

He laughs as he peers around me. "Thanks, but I'm pretty sure they only have kids' clothes back there."

I teasingly narrow my eyes and stick out my lower lip. "You're just jealous."

"I am," he agrees easily as we head toward the checkout. "What I wouldn't give for a unicorn sweatshirt of my own."

He sounds so genuinely bummed that I let out a stupidly girly giggle, but it can't be helped. This right here is reason number two hundred and twenty-eight in the list titled *Why I Like Heath Reilly*—he's funny.

He's not laugh-out-loud funny. He doesn't use jokes to call attention to himself or to impress anyone, like most guys I know. He just has this low-key sense of humor that never fails to make me smile, sometimes days later when I remember something I overheard him say.

We have enough cash from the couple we shared a ride with to cover our purchases and soon we're headed toward the motel, our hands weighed down by shopping bags.

It's not until after we check in and get our key that awkwardness rears its ugly head again. I'm not sure who starts slowing their pace first, but I swear we're walking so slowly we're practically inching our way toward the motel room.

For my part, anxiety is rising with every step. We pass by room after room on the ground floor, the numbers getting higher on the paint-chipped doors.

A motel room alone with Heath Reilly.

I don't know if I can handle this.

We pass an archway and I spot a pool in the courtyard beyond. I'm hit with the familiar scent of chlorine before we're continuing on to the next row of rooms.

Our row.

My muscles are aching with the urge to drop these bags and go for a dip in that pool. It's not hot out, but I'm warm from all the walking, and aside from that, this nervous energy needs an outlet.

This is not unusual for me. I'm a sporty kinda girl. I run track, I play tennis, I ski…and right now I'd give just about anything to work off this rising anxiety so it doesn't come out in the form of tears. Or worse, a panic attack.

But all too soon, we're standing in front of our room. "Lucky number thirteen," I mumble as I eye the gold number on the door.

He makes a little snorting sound of amusement. "Great. More bad luck."

He turns the key and throws open the door, stepping back to gesture grandly like he's the bellhop at the Ritz or something. "Madame," he says under his breath.

His teasing eases a little of the tension, but the moment we're alone in this room, I can't breathe. My brain is only capable of one thought that it shouts over and over again.

I am alone in a motel room with Heath Reilly!

I look around for something to ease this silence. A TV would be so helpful right about now. But no dice. There is a TV but there's also a piece of paper taped over it saying it's out of order. I do find an electrical outlet though so I busy myself with plugging in my phone and replying to texts that are now flooding my screen.

There are messages from a still-worried Noelle, a concerned Mr. Deckman, and about eighty all-caps messages from Mara that run the gamut from guilt at not picking up when I'd called earlier to worry about where I am and if I'm alive.

These are followed by a single text from Mara's mom, which makes me laugh.

"What's so funny?" Heath asks from behind me.

I turn to see him sprawled out on one of the beds. He's plugged his phone in too and is fussing with the buttons to try and get it to turn on.

I hold up my phone. "Mara's mom is threatening to call the National Guard."

He arches his brows. "How did Mara's mom get involved in this?"

I shake my head, still smiling as I reply to her and Mara's texts. "I love Mara's mom, but she tends to worry."

As soon as I say it, I remember the conversation he'd overheard with me and my parents, and the sympathy I'd seen in his eyes. I can feel his gaze on me now and I hate what he must be thinking.

"Not that my parents don't worry too," I lie.

He pinches his mouth shut as he nods. *I never said that*, his innocent expression seems to say.

And he *hadn't* said it. But he was thinking it.

"They're just..." I flounder and my gaze roams over the ugly watercolor prints on the wall and the threadbare duvets on our beds as I try to find the words to explain.

Not that he's asking for an explanation, but I don't like this nagging sensation that says he's feeling sorry for me. "They're just not involved," I finally say.

"I get that," he says slowly. "My parents aren't involved either. Too busy dealing with their own drama." He adds that last part with a cynical smirk that I've never seen from him before.

It makes me inexplicably sad.

I nod though, because at least he's not feeling sorry for me. "Mara's mom makes up for it in spades," I add, hoping to lighten the mood.

He grins again and my belly does a backflip in response. "Oh yeah?"

I nod, coming over to sit on the edge of my bed, the furthest my phone cord allows. "She had Mara when she was young, and she split with Mara's dad." I don't know why I'm telling him about Mara's family, but it's easier than talking about mine and he's watching me with interest. "So, it's just the two of them. Which I'm sure is hard," I say. "But it's nice to be around. She's so invested in Mara's life. And mine now, too, because I hang out at Mara's so often."

"That does sound nice," he says.

I look away because the way he's looking at me...

It makes my skin feel raw like I'm totally exposed. "My parents care too, of course." I blurt this out so suddenly, I feel a blush creeping up my neck. It sounds like I'm trying to convince somebody.

Like I'm trying to convince myself.

"I'm sure they do." He says it so gently I flinch.

I don't want his sympathy, and I'm irritated as hell that he overheard that phone call earlier.

"It's just..." I swallow hard. Why am I even trying to explain? What do I care if he thinks he knows my life? "They love me, obviously. But...they love each other, too," I say.

They love each other more.

I don't say it but I swear I can hear it hanging in the air between us. I'm afraid to look at Heath because I don't want to see that pity again.

"At least your parents get along," he says in this rueful tone that has me looking over.

He gives me a smile that's not pitying, just...filled with understanding. "Mine can't stand each other. They say they stay together for me and my brothers but I'm not sure they're doing us any favors."

"I'm sorry," I say.

He shrugs. "I'm used to it."

I arch my brows, unable to hide my disbelief.

"The trick is knowing what's gonna set off World War III," he says in that same wry tone, like this is all just a joke.

"And then avoiding those topics. That's what my parents do, most of the time."

"That sounds...unhealthy," I say. I try to soften it with a smile. "Not that I'm one to judge. I overheard my mom telling her friends that she'd never have another kid because it's too much of a distraction from their marriage."

The moment the words slip out, my eyes widen in horror. I have to stop myself from clapping a hand over my mouth. It's a true story—I'd heard her say that in third grade. But I've never told anyone about that. Not even Mara. And I have no idea why I just spilled that secret to Heath.

"Shit," Heath mutters. But again, there's no pity. If anything, he looks pissed.

On my behalf?

The thought makes me squirm as my chest tightens uncomfortably. I turn away, feigning more concentration than necessary as I respond to Noelle and Mr. Deckman with reassurances that we're safe and will be there by lunchtime tomorrow.

Assuming the train schedule I found online on my phone is up to date, this should be true.

The bed sinking is the first clue that Heath's come over to join me on my bed. I stiffen, turning to see that he's brought the bag of food with him and is sitting cross legged watching me.

When his gaze meets mine, he holds out a bag of tortilla chips. "Hungry?"

I nod and quickly snag the bag from him. "Starving," I admit.

I haven't eaten all day, and while I was afraid eating would make me sick, right now it works wonders to make me feel more human.

"Just think," he says. "This time tomorrow, you'll be in New York, your presentation completed and a raging success—"

I interrupt with a little huff of amusement at his optimism.

"And you'll be heading out for an amazing dinner with your friends at some awesome Manhattan restaurant," he continues.

I smile at the thought. "It feels so far away."

He nods. "But we'll get there."

I nod as well and suddenly swallowing is difficult because my throat gets way too tight.

We'll figure this out, he said earlier when I was ready to fall apart. *We can still make it.*

And now, *we'll get there.*

This guy makes 'we' sound so good. I can practically feel it wrapping around me, making me feel safe and cared for. *We* is the ultimate luxury. *We* is sipping hot cocoa in front of a warm fire after being out in the cold.

We is tempting.

I cough a little as I choke on the dry, salty chips.

We is exactly the sort of temptation I definitely can't afford.

I set down the bag of chips and shove those thoughts aside as I reach for a drink to wash down the chips. Because he's right—this time tomorrow we'll be surrounded by our friends and life will be back to normal. I won't have to deal with this temptation any more.

I take a deep breath. Which means now is the time to say what I should have said hours ago. "Hey, Heath?"

He looks up from the bag of jerky he's opening and those hazel eyes hold me hostage.

"I'm really glad you're here with me," I say. "And I'm grateful for your help. And...thank you." I clear my throat. "Thank you for staying."

EIGHT

Heath

MY HEART SLAMS against my ribcage and I don't even know why.

Her expression is so sweet. So sincere. So...scared?

That flicker of wariness is hidden deep, but I see it. After spending a day so close to her and without her being able to escape, I'm seeing a lot of things I've never noticed before.

And right now? She's wary as all hell even though she clearly means what she's saying.

I smile and murmur a *no problem*, but in my head all I can see is Noelle's text. *Stuck with Heath, of all people? Dude, that sucks.*

My smile fades fast as I try to reconcile that text with what she's saying right now.

Apparently Celia hates me...but she's grateful to me. She's stuck 'in hell' because she's with me, and yet she just opened up to me about personal stuff I know she doesn't share with just anyone.

How do I know?

I just do.

This girl might be outgoing and chatty, but there's a brick wall around her tiny frame and it's topped with barbed wire. I see that now. Or maybe I've always seen it. And maybe I'm the *only* one who's seen it because she doesn't do that whole bubbly, smiley routine with me.

That's given me an advantage, in one sense. She might not buy the hype about me, but I'm not buying what she's selling either.

A big part of me wants to ask her outright what her deal is with me—just get the question out of my head and out in the open once and for all. But when I go to do that now, I see the most vulnerable expression on her face, like admitting she's grateful to me meant opening a vein or something.

And I can't bring myself to do it.

But I'm also getting tired of being on the outside of this wall. If she's grateful to me, then great. That's nice, I guess. But I'm well aware that the moment we're in New York and she's surrounded by her friends again, I'll go back to being that guy she goes out of her way to avoid.

But until then? Well, until then she's stuck with me. And maybe it's time I make the most of that.

"So, your parents," I say as casually as I can as I reach for a handful of peanuts.

She stiffens. "What about them?"

I shrug, trying for nonchalance. I don't even know where I'm going with this. I just want to figure her out. I'm weirdly desperate to know what makes her tick, to understand why she's so hot and cold around me, and why she's scared to be in the same room with me when she also seems to understand that I'm not going to hurt her.

I throw some nuts in my mouth and chew, buying myself time. "That's got to be hard," I finally say.

She sits back and crosses her legs as she brushes off her hands, her lips curved down in a frown and her expression thoughtful. "Honestly, I'm not sure I know what a normal relationship looks like," she says slowly. "But I don't think what my parents have would be considered one."

For a second I think she's not going to say any more but after a pause, she adds, "They're incredibly codependent." Her lips curl up in disgust, though I don't think she even realizes she's doing it. She takes a deep breath and meets my gaze head on. "But I know they love me in their way, so it's fine."

She tosses her hair with a dismissive gesture like it's all meaningless. Her tone says that's all she's going to say on the subject.

I think about everything she's told me today. All the random little nuggets of insights about Celia that are shifting around in my brain like puzzle pieces that I can't seem to fit together. My mind snags on the memory of her looking and sounding so determined earlier…

I've never been in a relationship and I don't plan on being in one anytime soon. Not until college, at least.

"Are they why you refuse to date?" I ask suddenly.

She freezes in the middle of reaching for another chip, and her eyes glaze over like she's a deer in headlights. "What?"

I try not to smile, but she looks ridiculously cute, all shocked and put on the spot like this. "It would make sense," I say. "If they don't have a normal relationship, I mean."

Even as I say it, I know it's true. Her wide eyes, so freakin' scared—they just confirm it.

And my heart twists in my chest, because all at once I see it. She doesn't want to be codependent. She wants to give her presentation, and go to the college of her dreams, and she wants to do it all on her terms. No compromises or distractions.

Something settles in my chest with the realization. At least one small section of the puzzle comes into focus.

"Maybe," she hedges. And then, with a lift of her chin, "Yes. It's definitely because of them. Mainly my mom." And now that she's talking, words are spilling out of her like she can't stop them. "She used to have dreams, you know? Every once in a while she talks about them, but she gave it all up the day she met my dad. Suddenly her entire life became about making him happy and helping him to achieve his goals." She shakes her head, her brows drawn together. "I don't want that for myself."

I watch her for a long moment, my chest tugging and aching like whatever she's feeling, I can feel it too. Which isn't true, obviously. But I swear I can feel her frustration and her hurt echoing in my chest. "You know it doesn't have to be like that, right?"

She pauses in chewing and gives me a suspicious side eye that's so adorable, I can't stop a smile in return.

"I'm serious," I say. "Relationships aren't all bad. Or they don't have to be, at least."

She pops a peanut in her mouth and reaches for a club soda. "I'll take your word for it."

She's serious. The girl is one hundred percent serious about not getting involved with a guy, and that...annoys me.

My hands clench around the bag of chips in my hands before I shake off the irritation.

No, it doesn't *bother* me. Why would it?

It just *intrigues* me, that's all. Most girls I know are obsessed with who likes who and the whole relationship thing.

Hell, most guys I know are too.

"You really don't want to see what all the fuss is about?" I say in clear disbelief.

She lifts a shoulder. "I'll find out eventually. I'm not saying I'm going to stay single forever, just until I get my life sorted."

I arch my brows. "So, like, when you're forty?"

Her lips curve up and her eyes glint with laughter. "No, just...when I'm ready. Maybe college. Maybe after. Maybe never." She shrugs.

"I see." I try to sound serious but I fail.

She narrows her eyes. "What? Why do you seem so amused by this?"

"I'm not." I shake my head but I can't help the chuckle that escapes. "I'm not laughing at you," I say quickly. "I've just never met anyone so anti-romance, that's all."

"I'm not anti-romance," she mutters, her cheeks pink as she ducks her head, fixing her attention on a bag of candy she found in the bag.

"It sure sounds like it," I say. "You're like the Grinch of love."

She slumps forward so her elbows rest on her knees and she shakes her head with a rueful laugh at my teasing. "I am not."

Her hair has fallen forward so it's shielding her face, but I still see her pink cheeks. I'm embarrassing her, and I swear I don't mean to, but it's too fun to tease her.

"I am all for romance for other people," she adds, her

tone a touch defensive. "I just don't want it for myself yet, that's all."

"So, there's nothing you're curious about when it comes to relationships," I say, my tone goading. What I really want to say is, you've never gotten close to a guy and wanted more than friendship? You've really never wanted to be kissed? But I don't want to embarrass her any more than I already have so I stick with, "You've never felt like maybe you're missing out on something?"

She peeks up at me, and I see it. A flicker in her eyes, a pinching of her lips.

I lean back and point with a laugh. "Aha. There is something." I wave my fingers in a *bring-it-on* motion. "Come on, Cece. We're train buddies now. You can tell me."

She rolls her eyes, but she's smiling. "It's stupid."

"Say it," I insist.

I am weirded out by how much I want to hear whatever she's about to say. It could be anything, I don't care. I just want to know her secrets.

And yeah. That's super weird.

She clears her throat and takes a deep breath. "Valentine's Day."

I stare at her blankly. "What?"

She shrugs and her cheeks turn bright red. "I know, it's stupid."

"It's not stupid," I say quickly. "Just...Explain."

Her tongue flicks out to wet her lips and I try not to stare.

I try and fail.

One little gesture and now all I'm aware of are her lips, her scent...the fact that she and I are on a bed together. Alone.

"I guess there's some part of me that feels like I'm

missing out on Valentine's Day," she says quickly. "I mean, my friends and I always have a blast every year. We do a whole Galentine's Day thing, and it's great. But ever since I was little and we used to do those homemade valentines exchanges with those little mailboxes we made out of shoeboxes...?"

She glances over and I nod that I remember. It was a grade school thing—everyone wrote everyone else a valentine and stuffed them into each other's homemade mailboxes.

She shrugs. "Like I said, stupid."

"Not stupid," I say again.

She purses her lips and looks away.

"So, that's it then," I say, leaning forward to try and catch a glimpse of her expression. "Getting Valentine's Day cards is the only temptation?"

I don't even know why I'm pushing this. It has nothing to do with me if she wants to stay single for the foreseeable future.

She shrugs, and I get another surge of irritation because she's retreating again. There's something she's not saying.

"Come on," I tease, my tone wheedling. "Don't tell me you've never had a crush on someone."

She barely moves, but I hear her breath catch.

I'm right. She likes someone. Or she has at some point, at least.

My jaw locks and my muscles tense and—

What the hell is this?

My stomach churns and my chest tightens. and..

Jealousy.

Holy crap. This is freakin' *jealousy*, and it nearly knocks me on my ass.

It's completely unwarranted, and doesn't make any

sense whatsoever. I wasn't even jealous of Pamela and Dominic. I have no business being jealous of whatever guy Celia has the hots for.

But I find myself shifting closer to her end of the bed, and I feel her tense as I approach.

"Don't tell me you've never been tempted to break your own rules," I continue.

My tone's still teasing, but there's something different in the air between us. It's not nearly as light as it was before, and I wonder if she feels it too. It's an entirely new kind of tension and it has my gaze dropping to her lips.

"I bet, if the right guy asked you out, you'd say yes." I'm totally goading her now, and I don't know why.

For a second, I think she's not going to respond at all. But then she turns back to face me and those perfect, cupid's bow lips are set in a mocking smirk. "It's kinda funny that *you*, of all people, are arguing in favor of relationships after the way yours just ended."

Stuck with Heath, of all people?

Noelle's text flashes in my mind's eye, and I jerk back like I've just been smacked.

Celia's smirk is instantly replaced by a wince, and guilt fills her eyes. "Sorry. That was a low blow."

It's seriously not until that moment that Pamela pops into my head. All this talk of romance and relationships, and I've managed to completely blank on the girl who's been my on-again-off-again girlfriend for the past two years.

"No, you're right," I say. "I'm probably not one to talk."

She shifts, her gaze everywhere but on me. "I shouldn't have brought that up."

"It's fine," I say.

And it is. I've barely thought about Pamela since that humiliating phone call earlier today. I should be broken up about it, but I can't seem to care. I don't know how to say that aloud without sounding like a total dick, so I keep quiet.

We're both quiet except for the sounds of crunching and chewing for a few long seconds.

"I don't get why you keep getting back together with her." Celia's not facing me, but her tone makes it sound like the words were torn out of her. She hugs her arms over her chest and shakes her head. "Never mind, it's none of my business."

It's not. But watching her avoid my gaze, turning away from me...

I can practically see her retreating, fleeing from me even though she's still right here, on the same bed and within arm's reach.

"It's fine," I say. "I don't mind talking about it."

"It's really not my business," she says again.

I don't argue.

"I guess I don't get why you care." I say it as nicely as I can, but it's what I'm dying to figure out. She honestly seems upset on my behalf, which makes no sense given the way she acts around me.

"It's just..." She huffs. "You're a good guy, Heath. You deserve better."

You're a good guy...says the girl who's gone back to staring at me like I'm the big bad wolf.

"What I meant was," I say slowly. "I don't understand why you care when you so obviously don't like me."

Her head whips around and she's staring at me with wide eyes. "W-what?"

I let out a humorless huff of laughter at her shock. "I saw Noelle's text, Celia."

Her lips part, but she says nothing.

I shift on the bed, my chest tight and hot with frustration as I lean forward for a better look at her expression which is still partially hidden behind her hair. "I don't understand why you're worried about how Pamela treats me when being alone with me is apparently your version of hell on earth."

The silence that falls is so thick it makes me want to shout just to end it.

My hands clench against the bedspread and some part of me can't believe I actually confronted her about this.

I don't do confrontations, just like I don't do anger. I keep the peace. I smooth things over. I don't call girls out on the fact that they don't like me.

But here I am, and her answering silence only makes me more certain I need to know the answer. I'm desperate for an explanation and I can't ignore it any longer.

The silence is filled with tension...but this time, I swear to God I'm not going to be the one to break it.

NINE

Celia

MY HEART IS RACING SO QUICKLY I can't quite catch my breath.

My leg muscles are twitching with the urge to run, but Heath's gaze is holding me in place. This thick tension is weighing me down like an anchor.

I start to move, but he frowns like I'm disappointing him.

"I, um...I don't know what you mean," I say, dipping my head as I edge toward the end of the bed and stand.

"Seriously?" He sounds so jaded, and I don't like it. "You're going to pretend you didn't see Noelle's text?"

I don't answer. I'm too busy pacing the small room, trying to find something to occupy my hands, to distract us both, to...

Oh, I don't know what I'm looking for. All I know is I can't just sit there while the guy I've liked since second grade glares at me and accuses me of hating him.

I have no idea what to do with that, and I definitely have no clue what I'm supposed to say.

I stop near the door. The urge to run is very, very real.

But where? I'm in a freakin' strange town. It's dark outside and I have no idea where we are or how safe this neighborhood is.

"Please don't run away from me." It's the exhaustion in his voice that makes me still, and then has me turning around to face him.

He's sitting on the edge of the bed now, his arms flung out wide like he's showing me he's not concealing any weapons. The look in his eyes is equally weary and resigned. "Look, I don't know what I ever did to you," he starts.

"Nothing," I say quickly. "You never did anything."

He stares at me and I can't read his eyes. "So you just don't like me because I rub you the wrong way or something?" He scrubs the back of his neck. "I guess I can understand that."

He sounds uncertain.

He sounds...hurt.

My heart cracks. This is killing me.

He might honestly be the nicest guy I know. I never meant to hurt his feelings. It wasn't his fault I had the crush to end all crushes. He couldn't help it that he was so dang wonderful.

But what am I supposed to say? He's still watching me like he's waiting for some sort of response and my mind is a total blank. I'm racking my brain for any reasonable, logical excuse, but I'm coming up empty.

It's never even occurred to me that he might have noticed the way I avoid him. He's never said anything about it before.

He's never even seemed to notice me before, least of all care about how I act around him.

"Is there something I can do to make you more...comfortable around me?" he asks.

And that right there is the last straw.

Why, God? Why does he have to be so freakin' kind on top of everything else? Why does he have to be good and nice and thoughtful as well as hot? It's too much. It's not right.

His brows are arched like he's waiting for a response. Is there anything he can do?

"No," I whisper.

His face falls and I feel a stab of regret. But it's the truth.

If our day together has taught me anything, it's this. There's nothing he can do to make me stop having these feelings for him. I'll never not find him attractive. I'll never not wonder what it would be like if he kissed me. I'll never not find his humor funny or his humility endearing or his kindness charming.

"There's *nothing* I can do," he repeats, disbelief in his voice because what I'm saying is unbelievably rude.

But it's true. After today it's clearer than ever. There is nothing he can do to make me stop wanting him, and that...that scares the freakin' crap out of me.

I start backing up again, my heart in my throat as panic surges through me with a jolt of adrenaline.

"No," I say again.

Wrong answer.

His face falls...and I'm the worst.

He's off the bed now, standing and stalking toward me. He's not dangerous. I'm not afraid he's going to hurt me.

But I *am* scared.

Because when he's close, I lose control. I lose my senses. I lose *myself*.

"Don't," I say, backing up until my back is pressed against the door.

He stops. Of course he does. He's too kind to ever intentionally scare anyone, least of all a girl.

He stands there, halfway between the bed and me, his brows furrowed and his eyes filled with concern and hurt. I watch his jaw work. I see his throat move when he swallows. He holds up his hands, palms out. "Celia, I don't understand why you're so scared of me."

I don't answer because I have no idea how to explain that without telling him the truth.

"I am so grateful for your help today," I start.

He makes a scoffing sound in disbelief, and I can't blame him. That came out way too stilted and formal. I wince as I try to think of a way to rephrase.

Because the thing is, as much as I don't want him to know the embarrassing truth about my crush on him...I also really don't want to hurt his feelings.

Too late.

But with every second his gaze holds mine and I see just how badly I hurt him, I feel this clawing sensation in my chest, like the truth is trying to get out.

But what am I going to say? *It's not you, it's me?*

That sounds too lame for words.

"I *am* grateful," I try again.

"So, you're grateful but you can't stand me?" he says.

"That's not..." I press back against the door as he takes another step toward me. "That's not what the text meant."

His brow furrows even more and there's a hint of anger in his eyes now. "You hate me, Celia. You basically admitted it."

"I don't hate you," I say quickly, words tumbling out of my mouth because... Crap, he really thinks I *hate* him?

"I don't hate you," I say again. "Far from it."

Far from it.

The words seem to echo in the air, but all I can actually hear is our breathing.

I said too much, and I know it. But there's no calling those words back now, so all I can do is wait.

For a long second he stares at me in disbelief, but I swear I see the moment when it clicks. When he understands.

My stomach sinks with mortification even as my heart jolts into action.

His hazel eyes go from narrowed with suspicion to wide with surprise. But it's the way they darken that makes my pulse turn into a flutter.

As I watch his eyes grow heavy and dark and...dangerous.

And when he moves closer—slowly, so very slowly—I'm afraid my heart is going to beat right out of my chest.

"Celia," he says slowly, his voice filled with meaning. His gaze drops to my lips and I forget how to breathe.

I've seen his eyes warm with kindness and affection, I've seen them filled with frustration and even a hint of anger. I've seen them hurt and confused. But this look in his eyes is different from anything I've seen from him.

He's so close now that I can feel the heat of his body as I press back against the door.

"Celia," he says my name again, gently this time, like he's trying to calm me or soothe me.

"I can't," I say quickly.

Not even I know what I mean by that. I can't admit it

aloud? I can't have this conversation? I can't let myself like you?

All of the above, I guess.

This new, heavy-lidded gaze rakes over me and I swear he sees everything now. I am fully clothed but I might as well be naked because the way he's looking at me makes me want to run and hide.

He knows.

He knows that I like him.

Oh dear God, what have I done?

I turn and throw open the door before I can stop to think. "Gonna go for a swim. I'll be back in a bit," I say.

It's a lame excuse. We both know I'm just running away. Avoiding the inevitable.

But that's fine by me. This is a conversation I've been avoiding for years now. I am all for avoidance.

So I run barefoot out to the pool area, which is blessedly empty, but still lit and stocked with thin white towels.

I quickly shed my clothes until I'm down to my underwear. Thanks to not being blessed in the curves department, my black boy shorts and bralette can totally pass for a swimsuit, especially in the dark. And soon enough I'm in the water, the cold a welcome shock.

The laps I swim are exactly what I need to work off this frantic state. I'm not the world's best swimmer, but I slice through the water with as much force as I can muster. My mind stops racing after a few laps, and a few more after that I pause in the deep end and come up for air.

Mistake.

I shouldn't have stopped. I mean, I would have gotten a cramp and maybe drowned if I didn't take a breather, but at least I wouldn't have realized that Heath has followed me out here.

That he's watching me.

That the dark intensity in his eyes is still there and it is fixed on me without a hint of apology.

"You ready to talk yet?" he asks in that low, mild voice of his, which at the moment seems at odds with the fierce stare he's got going on.

"Um..." I say.

Very eloquent, obviously. But no. I'm not ready to talk. Especially because... "There's nothing to talk about."

There. I said something. I take a deep breath, way more proud of myself than that stupid comment warrants.

He arches a brow like he's thinking the same thing. "Nothing, huh?"

I shake my head, keenly aware that I am wet. And nearly naked. And on full display thanks to the pool lights that have turned the water into a well-lit blue lantern in the middle of the dark courtyard.

I hear sounds from a TV coming from one of the rooms nearby, but that's it. There's no one out here but me and Heath.

Heath, who's frowning at me.

Heath, who's crossing his arms over his chest like he's trying to show off his muscles.

Heath, who says, "Celia, if you don't come out of there and finish this conversation, I'm coming in."

My jaw drops. I've definitely never heard him talk like that before—like he means business. Not mean, but stern.

"Um, what?" I start.

But he's already starting to shed his clothes and when he's down to his boxers, he dives in.

I'm still gaping when he surfaces and shoves wet hair off his face.

He flashes me the sexiest grin I've ever seen in my life

before swimming toward me, not stopping until he's right in front of me. He comes out of the water just enough to brace his arms on either side of me so I can't escape.

Crap. I scowl at him and that makes him grin again.

I hate that grin.

My heart, however, loves it. The dang organ breaks into a freakin' cha-cha at the sight of it and my belly is swarming with butterflies.

Crap, crap, double crap. This reaction right here? This is exactly why I keep my distance. The guy is dangerous.

His gaze narrows on me. "What is going on in that head of yours?" He murmurs it so softly it's almost like he's talking to himself.

I'm holding the edge of the pool with one hand and I start to kick before realizing his legs are so close that trying to kick will have me rubbing up against him in all sorts of inappropriate ways.

I swallow hard.

I'm stuck. I am quite literally trapped. But before I can say as much, Heath eases back a bit. "Sorry, I'm not trying to scare you."

I blink at the regret that tightens his expression.

"I'm not scared of you," I say.

He gives a humorless huff of laughter.

"I'm not scared you'd hurt me," I amend.

He studies me and then nods in acknowledgement. "Fair enough. But I still don't like to see you scared."

I shrug, suddenly feeling more helpless than I can ever remember. "Like I said, there's nothing you can do about it."

His inhale is sharp. And whatever he sees when he's staring at me so intently like this, it makes him groan and his head falls back for a second like he's praying for patience.

When he drops his head again, he's so close I can feel his breath against my wet skin.

I hate it and I love it all at once.

I want him closer even as the reasonable part of my brain screams to run.

This is exactly what I've been trying to avoid, because when he's this close? I can't think.

When he's this close, I can't even breathe.

"Celia Kennedy," he says slowly, his voice gruff and deep. "Do you like me?"

My lips part and my skin is on fire everywhere his gaze lands. My cheek, my nose, my chin, my neck.

Do you like me?

Is he serious?

He has to know that I do. That I have for as long as I can remember.

He moves in a little closer, his gaze now locked on my lips. "Celia?"

"Yes?" It's little more than a squeak.

"I"m going to kiss you," he says, his voice low, calm, reassuring.

"Um..."

A hint of a smile plays over his lips as he drags his gaze up to mine. "If you don't want me to, just say so."

If you don't want me to...?

Is he serious?

I've dreamt of him kissing me for so long I can't even remember when the fantasies began.

He's waiting for an answer as he moves in slowly.

So, so slowly.

"Um," I say again. And that's all I say.

And then I can't say anything because his lips meet mine, and I forget my own name.

I forget who I am and why this is so wrong.

Sensations hit me so hard and fierce, they steal my breath and my lips part with a gasp. He groans in response, and I feel it because his bare chest is pressed to mine and I would drown if he hadn't wrapped an arm around me to keep me afloat, trapping me between him and the pool's edge.

Even in this cold water, I am on fire.

He tilts his head, and with firm but gentle caresses he coaxes my lips apart, teasing and tasting with each new graze of his mouth over mine.

My head is above water but I could drown in this kiss.

Somewhere deep in the dark recesses of my brain a voice is saying this is wrong. It's so wrong.

But I ignore the voice and focus on the feel of his lips pressed to mine, his breath that heats my lips, his arms and his hands that hold me steady, in this kiss...

This kiss that feels so freakin' right.

TEN

Heath

I SHOULD END THIS.

I know I should end this kiss. We're going too fast and I'm losing all control.

But I can't stop.

Her lips are soft beneath mine, her breath coming in sweet little gasps that have my heart thudding painfully against my ribcage. I knew I was attracted to Celia, but nothing could have prepared me for the jolt of lightning that struck the moment my lips met hers.

Even as I kiss her, I'm reeling from it—the instant heat, the raging desire, the intense connection that seems to wind around us making it impossible for me to let her go.

And I *should* let her go.

Instead, I move in closer. I'm pressed against her, one arm tight around her waist and the other braced on the edge, keeping us afloat.

Her kiss is pure passion as she tilts her head and

matches my movements, her lips clinging and grazing over mine like she can't get enough.

I know I definitely can't get enough.

One kiss will not be enough. I know this like I know I need air to breathe. My list of needs in life just grew to include Celia's kiss. Food, water, air...and *this*.

Celia makes this little whimpering sound that drives me insane. I don't care who can see us or where we are. I don't care about how we got here or where we're going. Her hands are on my chest, her fingers curling into me, but now she slides her arms up and around my neck and I groan at the new contact.

When I lift my head, she gasps for air. The kiss has gotten so out of control, I'm barely giving her a chance to breathe.

Slow down.

Instead, I trail my lips to her jaw and kiss my way down her neck, which is dripping with pool water but still hot to the touch.

Her scent is intoxicating.

The girl feels like heaven.

The sound of a motel room door closing somewhere nearby has her tensing in my arms, her fingernails digging into my shoulders.

Crap.

I got too carried away.

I pull back slowly, looking down into her dark, dazed eyes. Her cheeks are flushed, her lips swollen...

She is the most beautiful sight I've ever seen.

I struggle to draw in air. Oh hell. What is happening to me right now? My chest is way too tight, and it's not just desire. It's warmth, and tenderness, and—

Crap. I don't know what this is.

Her lips are still parted, but she blinks a few times and I see her tumble back to reality.

I brace myself for it. That wariness. That fear.

But all I see right now is a shy little smile and a vulnerability in her eyes that brings out protective instincts I didn't even know I had. I reach a hand up to touch her cheek, brushing wet hair back behind her ear. "You okay?" I ask.

She nods. I know that's the only answer I'm going to get for now so I let her go gently, helping her to the edge where she lifts herself out. I follow, snagging a few of the thin, white towels that are stacked nearby and toss her a couple.

I do my best not to notice her body, I swear.

Not just because I'm a gentleman like that, but because I'm not sure I can survive a night sleeping in the same room with this girl with that image in my head.

When she's all wrapped up in towels and I've tugged some clothes back on, we head back to the room.

She heads straight for the bathroom to take a shower, and as I wait for her to be done, I lay back in my bed and I think.

Celia Kennedy likes me.

It's only one thought, really, but everything it signifies keeps my brain occupied. I find myself replaying every interaction I've had with Celia over the years with this new information, and it reshapes every memory. It casts every look and every word in a new light. The way she's avoided me. Why she's so scared around me...

My heart is a mangled wreck by the time she slips out of the bathroom in that ridiculous purple unicorn sweatshirt and a pair of track pants she'd found at the store, her hair falling wet down her back.

She takes one look at me and darts over to her bed,

sliding under the covers and pulling them up to her chin, blushing all the while.

I start to laugh. I can't help it. The Celia I know is not shy. Not around anyone else, at least. And even around me, I never saw shy. Wary and reluctant as she did her best to avoid me? Yes. But not shy.

This side of her is just too stinkin' cute.

"Don't laugh at me," she mutters from her bed.

"I'm not," I say quickly.

She turns her head to glare over at me, but there's a flicker of amusement in her eyes. "You are."

"Only a little."

Her cheeks get even pinker and she presses her lips together.

Ah hell. She's actually embarrassed. I go up onto one elbow so I can lay on my side and face her. "Celia?"

She ignores me, turning her head so she's staring at the ceiling instead.

"Cece," I tease.

Her lips quirk, but she doesn't respond.

"I swear I'm not laughing at you." I'm *definitely* not laughing at the fact that she likes me. That she has liked me for…for how long?

I suck in a deep breath as my heart takes an unexpected tumble.

I have so many questions. How long has she felt this way? How did I not know?

And what would I have done if I had?

The answer seems so blazingly obvious. There's no doubt in my mind. I would have asked her out. I would have asked her out and been happy as hell if she'd said yes.

Would she have said yes though? The urge to laugh

fades fast as I remember her declaration that she doesn't do relationships.

"Hey," I say quietly, no hint of teasing this time.

She turns her head to face me.

"I'm not laughing at you," I say. "I just think it's sweet that you're shy around me now, that's all."

Her lips curve up slightly in a reluctant smile. "Yeah, well, this is all new to me, remember?"

My heart takes a dive toward the floor and I swallow hard. "Celia, have you ever..." I clear my throat. "Have you ever been kissed before?"

"Of course," she says promptly.

"Oh. Right." I nod, like that was a given.

This is *not* disappointment making my gut sink. And it's definitely not jealousy, because that would be totally insane, not to mention inappropriate.

"Jeremy Johnson," she says, a hint of laughter in her voice as she peeks over at me. "Spin the bottle at Noelle's birthday party."

I fall back against my pillow with a huff of amusement. Jeremy Johnson moved away in junior high. "So that would have been around..."

"Sixth grade," she supplies.

I look over to see that she's turned her head so she's looking at me. Her dark eyes glitter with self-deprecating laughter. "Be honest. How obvious was it that I didn't know what I was doing?"

I shake my head. "Not obvious at all."

She grins and I feel it in my chest.

"You're a natural," I tell her.

She giggles and the sound has me grinning like a fool.

A second passes with us just looking at each other, and I

find myself wondering what this means. "Should we, uh..." I arch my brows. "Should we talk about this?"

She blinks a few times before shaking her head. The flicker of panic was brief, but it was there. "Not yet."

I nod. She needs time to process. I can respect that. And besides, I literally just got out of a relationship today. I shouldn't be jumping into anything new.

I swear she's reading my mind because her brows draw down a little and she says softly, "You and Pamela..."

"Are done," I say quickly.

Her smile is rueful and a little sad. "I think I've heard that before."

I can't deny it. I want to open my mouth to say 'it's for real this time' or something to that effect but I feel like it'll sound hollow. Like I'm just saying that to make her feel better about the fact that we just made out in a pool.

But it *is* true. I don't know why I've let myself slip up and repeat my mistakes in the past, but I'm done with that now.

She's quiet for so long that I wonder what she's thinking about. She has a little crease between her brows like she's worried.

About me and Pamela?

I clear my throat. "I should never have gotten back together with her in the first place," I admit.

She bites her lip and then glances over at me. "So, why did you?"

That's the question of the century right there. And for once, I make myself face it. She deserves a real answer after everything that just went down between us. "I guess..." I pause because I have no idea where to start. "It's just easy, I guess."

I risk a look over and see her frowning in confusion.

I wince. "That sounds terrible, doesn't it?"

"Kinda," she says.

I chuckle a little at her honesty and then throw up my hands. "Honestly, I don't know why I keep doing this to myself. I genuinely liked Pamela two years ago, the summer we first got together. She was fun and easy to be around…"

I swallow hard and try not to fidget with the covers beneath me as I realize I'm telling the girl I just made out with about the girl who just dumped me.

Nope, nothing awkward about this situation.

"But those feelings faded quickly," I continue. "For both of us. It was pretty obvious right off the bat that we're like oil and water. But we stayed together because…because it was comfortable. Even when it wasn't comfortable at all."

I scrub a hand over my face because this isn't coming out right. "Sorry," I mumble. "I've never tried to explain this to anyone before."

"No," she says slowly. "I think I can sort of understand. Familiarity is comforting."

I shrug. "I guess. And then there's the fact that she's just as messed up as I am."

I hear her turn her head to look at me.

It's possible that came out sounding more jaded than intended.

"Not to badmouth Pamela," I add. "But I think we were both looking for something with each other. We didn't find it, and we should have just moved on, but we don't know how."

"So you'll just keep getting back together and hurting each other until you're both dead?" Her voice holds enough amusement that I know she's mostly joking.

"No. I mean it when I say I'm done." But even though

she was clearly teasing, her words keep circling in my head. They're hitting a nerve, or maybe jarring memories.

Silence falls and I start to wonder if she's drifted off.

"Hey, Heath?" she asks quietly. Almost a whisper.

I turn to look at her, and I'm pretty sure I'm a goner when I find her wide eyes gazing back at me so sweetly in the dark. "You okay?" she asks.

I take a deep breath. "Yeah. Just thinking."

I should stop talking. She doesn't need to hear the details about me and Pamela. Not when I have every intention of repeating that kiss at the earliest opportunity.

"About?" she asks.

I turn onto my side again to face her. "I don't want to end up like my parents either."

She doesn't say anything for a long while, but I know that she gets it. This thing between me and Pamela? It's everything I hate about my parents' relationship. There's no talking—not about anything real, at least. It's miserable but comfortable. It's companionship with someone who's just as messed up as you are so you don't have to try.

"You won't," Celia says suddenly.

I arch my brows at her certainty.

"You're too smart for that," she says.

"Thanks." I open my mouth to assure her that she won't be like her parents either, but I shut it again quickly.

She knows that already.

She's ensured that she won't be like them by staying far away from anyone who might tempt her to forget her goals.

That's why she's stayed away from me.

The thought is both heartwarming and terrifying, and I don't know what to make of it.

One kiss does not mean she's about to change her mind about being in a relationship.

And is that what I even want?

I swallow hard. I'm not ready to go there. Celia's right. I need to deal with Pamela and my own crap first before I can even think about this thing between us.

But if I did clear up this mess with Pamela? If I were ready to move on? Would I want to move on with Celia?

My stomach twists and my heart dives. I'm standing on the edge of a cliff and I can't tell if I'm about to soar or plummet.

I fall back against my pillow with a harsh exhale.

I can admit that the idea of being with Celia scares the crap out of me. She'd have expectations. She'd want to talk. She'd be...

Well, she'd be an actual girlfriend and not just a warm body at my side to keep me company at parties.

I flinch at the thought. Was that all Pamela was to me? Not at first, maybe. But this last time around, I'd been going through the motions. I'd known deep down that there were no real feelings there, not on either side. So why had I taken her back?

My gut twists as I realize I don't want to think about the answer. She'd been using me. I know that. But I guess I'd been using her too, in my own way.

Familiarity is comforting, Celia said.

I stare up at the ceiling.

Familiarity is safe.

I scrub a hand over my face. Pamela might have cheated, but I'm starting to realize I owe her an apology. A big one.

But as for me and Celia...

Even if I wanted something real—would she?

I turn to look at her and see that she's staring intently up at the ceiling, no doubt lost in her own thoughts.

"You worried about tomorrow?" I ask.

She nods. Her lips are shut tight and her hands are clutching the blankets in that grip of steel I know so well.

"We should get to sleep," I say. We have to be up early if we're going to catch that first train. I know without having to ask that Celia's already set her alarm.

"I know," she says with a sigh. "But I don't know if I can."

I have a feeling it's not just fears about her presentation tomorrow that have her looking so petrified, but I'm just as certain she doesn't want to talk about it.

"Why don't you rehearse your speech for me again," I say.

She scoffs. "That's nice of you, but I'm sure you don't want to hear that whole presentation again."

I smile up at the ceiling. "Actually, I was kind of hoping you'd bore me to sleep."

A pillow lands on my face and I laugh.

I hear her laughter too as I swat it away, and then she's on her side, a big grin on her face as she tells me I asked for it. With a deep breath, she launches into her speech...and I'm not bored in the slightest.

I realize I could listen to this girl talk about just about anything and enjoy the hell out of it.

When she's done, we talk about what she's going to say to the dean, which turns into a conversation about what plans I have for college—never a fun topic for me so it doesn't last long—and from there the conversation takes on a life of its own.

At some point, I get out of my bed and go to hers, though I'm careful to stay on top of the covers.

I am painfully aware that all of this is new to Celia. The

last thing I want to do is give her an actual reason to look at me with that wariness again. Or worse, fear.

So I keep my hands to myself, only giving in to the occasional kiss on top of her head when she slowly gets comfortable at my side.

The talking goes on all night, and when we finally do drift off, her snug in my arms, the sky is already starting to lighten with the sunrise.

ELEVEN

Celia

I FEEL LIKE DEATH.

I'm pretty sure I look worse.

But we make the train the next morning, and even get two seats together for the long ride into Manhattan.

The only good thing about having stayed up all night talking is that we're both too exhausted to talk much on the train. We spend most of it sleeping instead.

And if it's still weird to me that I'm now comfortable sleeping with my head on a unicorn-sweatshirt pillow in Heath's lap, I'm determined not to think about it. His hand is heavy on my shoulder, and it's nice. It's like a weighted blanket. And between his warmth, the sound of his steady breathing, and the rocking of the train as we head toward Manhattan, I start to drift off quickly.

Which is good because I'm desperate for sleep. Right now I need sleep more than I need to unwind all the thoughts spiraling through my head over what transpired the night before.

When I wake a while later, I feel semi-human again. I sit up and stretch, trying to be quiet because Heath is dead to the world beside me. My heart does an erratic tap dance against my rib cage at the sight of him like this.

You'd think after all this alone time, I'd be over it right? Like, how much time does one need to spend with one's crush before one is inoculated against these kinds of side effects?

Apparently for me, twenty-four hours isn't enough.

Not even kissing my crush has made me less aware of him physically.

I sneak another glance over at his absurdly hot profile—seriously, who looks so hot while passed out on a train?

Heath does, that's who. He's got a little stubble from not shaving, and his hair is all mussed bedhead. His straight nose and strong jaw are basically showing off right now at this angle. And his lips...

I swallow hard as I look away.

I can't be thinking about his lips right now. Because lip-thoughts will lead to kiss-thoughts and there is no place for that in my brain at the moment. Maybe later I'll have some peace and quiet to replay that epic kiss and make sense of all the feelings it stirred up in me.

Maybe sometime after that I'll even be able to put it into words.

And maybe at some point in the future, I'll actually figure out what it means.

Or if it means anything at all.

I glance over at Heath again and this time I studiously ignore the wild fluttering in my chest. I smooth down my skirt and fold the ugly sweatshirt in my lap.

Later. There'll be time to sort through these feelings later.

Right now it's more important than ever that I keep my priorities straight. And my priorities do not include boys. Not even the one beside me who may or may not have been the star of every silly romantic fantasy I've harbored since I was eight years old.

Nope. The only thing that matters right now is getting to the hotel in time for the solo presentations. I shift to straighten my blouse, frowning at the knotted mess my hair has become when I try to run my fingers through it.

Correction. The most important thing now is to get to the hotel *before* the solo presentations start so I don't show up looking like I've been up all night and am wearing clothes from the day before.

Heath doesn't stir for the next hour, and I sort of hate how relieved I am that I don't have to talk to him.

Don't get me wrong. I had a great time talking to him the night before. We talked about everything and nothing, and it was...

Well, it was like something straight out of one of my romantic fantasies. Snuggled up in his arms and talking like we're actually intimately acquainted and not just classmates who sometimes hang in the same crowd.

It was magic.

It was perfection.

It was...not reality. And neither was that kiss.

Both were clearly the result of a crazy day together. Too much alone time, combined with exhaustion and stress. It was a temporary anomaly. Obviously. And we'd be back to normal once we rejoined our friends and classmates.

I glance over at Heath's expression, which manages to be all sexy and broody even in sleep. With a sigh I pull out my notecards and go over the new presentation in my head. Or...I try to.

It's really not as easy as I'd like to forget about that kiss. Or the way it had felt to wake up in his arms. Or the way he'd talked so openly last night about so many different topics.

A knot of apprehension forms in my belly. It was one thing to have a crush on a guy I only really knew from afar. I wasn't sure I could handle a crush on a guy I'd kissed, and snuggled, and talked to.

Giving my head a shake, I try to focus on the cards in my hands. I am *this* close to wowing the dean of the college of my dreams. I am hours away from potentially having an interview.

This is so not the time to lose focus.

Heath finally wakes as we're heading into the tunnel that enters into Grand Central. He rubs a hand over his face with a yawn as he blinks his eyes open and turns from the dark tunnel outside our window to face me. "I slept through the whole thing?"

His smile is so sheepish, so boyish and adorable...

Gah! How is anyone supposed to concentrate on anything with him around?

"We should be arriving any minute now," I say. "From there it's a quick cab ride to the hotel."

He takes my hand when the train comes to a halt like it's the most natural thing in the world. Since we don't have luggage, we're the first off the train and Heath hauls me along beside him toward the crowded escalators. We both come to a halt when we reach the main level.

My jaw actually drops open at the sight of the constellations painted overhead and the sheer grandeur and bustle that is Grand Central Station.

"Whoa," I mutter.

He flashes me another grin that ought to be illegal for how cute it is. "This place is amazing."

He's all lit up with excitement, and I feel it too. As we veer into the thick crowd to reach the exit, I swear it's palpable. There's an energy around us, like a hum in the air. I can feel my pulse quickening and my lips curving up in a grin.

When we burst out onto the streets of Midtown Manhattan, a laugh tumbles out of me. And even though I couldn't explain the cause of that laugh to save my life, Heath seems to get it and he gives me a knowing grin. "Come on," he says, tugging on my hand. "I see a taxi line down this way."

I follow along where he's heading, but there's a second—just one heartbeat—when I find myself wishing we could skip the taxi and just keep walking. There's this little voice in my head that's urging me to skip the presentations, too, and just explore. Have fun. Take advantage of the fact that for a little while, at least, I have Heath all to myself.

For a second there, it's like a complete stranger has taken residence in my body and she's shouting for me to do something crazy and adventurous for once.

But I shut that voice down and follow Heath instead. At least Heath still has his head on straight. He's veering toward the front of the line with dogged determination. When we slide into the backseat of a cab and give the name of the hotel, he turns to me with a lopsided grin as his shoulders visibly relax. "I told you we'd get you there on time."

"You were right," I say with a smile.

He *had* made that promise. He'd made all kinds of promises when he had no reason to.

He didn't owe me anything.

I turn to look out the window because...he still doesn't.

He owes me nothing, and I hope he knows that. Last night was a mistake and I don't want him thinking that just because I've had a crush on him, he needs to be all chivalrous and noble or something.

The thought has me shifting uncomfortably in my seat. Apparently Heath misunderstands because he reaches for my hand in my lap and gives it a squeeze. "It's just a little traffic. We'll still be there in plenty of time."

I nod and force another smile. I'm watching the street signs pass, slowly but surely. We're not exactly whizzing through crosstown traffic, but we don't have far to go either.

We finally pull up to the hotel and I hand over my mother's poor, beleaguered credit card to the driver.

Heath's already hopping out and then he's opening my car door for me because...of course he is. I can't hold back a sigh as he reaches in and helps me out like I'm some delicate flower who needs to be escorted in and out of cars.

It's so sweet, but so different from how he's always treated me that it puts me on edge. He presses a hand lightly to my back as we head for the main doors, his body angled toward mine like he's ready to protect me from the crowds on the sidewalk. And then we reach the glass doors of the hotel, where—you guessed it. He opens the freakin' door for me.

I honestly have a moment where I'm not sure whether I'm about to laugh or cry. I have nothing against chivalry, it's just that seeing this side of him...all protective and thoughtful?

How the heck am I supposed to get over this crush? I mean, seriously. It was bad enough before when I just had to see his kind smile from afar and hear his voice from a distance.

And then there was the whole knight in shining armor routine from the day before. But now this?

I definitely cannot handle this. He's acting like I mean something to him, and that's just too much to absorb.

I'm actually relieved when we enter and find the entrance crowded with students from the conference. There are other tourists mingling about too, but the high-ceilinged, modern lobby is filled with our classmates, including Noelle.

"You made it!" My friend no sooner shouts the words before she's peeling away from some of our other friends and throwing herself on top of me.

I squeeze my friend hard in return, and that's when it happens.

Tears.

Stupid, ridiculous tears that I can't even explain spring to my eyes as she holds me tight and murmurs about how worried they'd all been.

I catch Heath's gaze over her shoulder as he's doing the whole bro-clap on the back move with Elijah and some of the other guys.

But even though he's smiling and responding to whatever they're saying, his gaze is fixed on mine. And he sees way too much.

He sees...everything.

I see his smile fade and his brows draw down in concern before I squeeze my eyes shut and tighten my grip around Noelle's waist. "Can we go get changed?" I ask. "I have to be at the presentation in twenty minutes."

"Of course, sweetie. Come with me." She shouts something to Elijah and Heath and the others about meeting up with them later and punches the button for the elevator.

The doors are sliding closed when I hear Heath shout out, "Good luck, Celia!"

The elevator doors are shut so I can't respond. Instead, I sink back against the elevator walls and watch the numbers tick by with a sigh.

Noelle shifts so she's standing in front of me with a narrowed gaze. A natural beauty, Noelle is one of those lucky girls who's strikingly gorgeous no matter what. Right now her long black hair is tossed up in a messy bun and her dark skin has no makeup whatsoever—and yet she still looks like a model. All high cheekbones, full lips, and almond-shaped eyes.

Eyes that are currently taking me in from head to toe.

"Quick shower first while I pick out your clothes..." She glances at the oversized watch she's sporting. "Then on the way to the presentations you can start."

"Start what?" I ask.

She smiles. "Talking, sweetie." The elevator doors open with a ding and she pushes me out into the hallway with a nudge. "You have a lot of talking to do."

TWELVE

Heath

"SO," Elijah says as we eventually break away from the other guys and head toward the elevators. "You gonna tell me what happened between you two?"

I scrub the back of my neck. "I don't know what you mean."

"Don't even try to lie, man," Elijah says with an easy grin. "I caught that look back there." He nods toward the lobby. "Not to mention the way you were all..."

He stops talking to hover all over me like an idiot, putting a hand to my back, fawning like a lovesick puppy until I shove him away with an exasperated laugh. "Shut up."

Elijah shrugs, holding his hands up in mock defense. "Just calling it like I see it. And I've gotta say..." He pulls back to eye me with open suspicion. "I've never seen you like that before."

I frown, looking away as we head into the next available elevator.

I can't pretend that I don't know what he's talking about, but I can't explain it either. I'm not that guy. I've never been some doting, overprotective, alpha dude who makes a show out of claiming his girl.

But that's totally what I did. I took one look at the other guys in the lobby and put a hand on her back in a silent *back off, she's mine* move. I can't even deny that's what it was because those were the exact words that went through my mind when I touched her.

Back off. She's mine.

I let out a loud exhale.

And was I hovering? Maybe.

Okay, definitely. But she's small and this city is big and—

Ah crap. What the hell is happening to me?

I rub my eyes. It's exhaustion, that's all. Even with that nap in the train, I'm all out of sorts. Ever since I woke to find Celia sleeping in my arms like a freakin' fairytale princess come to life, all sweet and innocent and way too pretty for the real world and—

And yeah. I just compared Celia to a freakin' fairytale princess, so okay. Wow. "This is bad."

I didn't actually mean to say it aloud, but I get a hand on the shoulder along with Elijah's laughter in response.

"Dude, what happened?" he asks.

I shake my head and drop my hand. "I have no idea."

Which is a lie, of course. I kissed her. That's what happened. I kissed Celia Kennedy.

And all I can think about is doing it again. It's all I thought about as we took turns getting changed at the motel this morning. It was all I thought about on the walk to the train station.

Hell, I dreamt about it on the train.

But that's not the worst part. Oh no. The worst part is, all these daydreams and fantasies? They weren't just about kissing. It was more. It was so much more. It was staying up late with her every night, even if it's just talking on the phone. It was visions of being able to hold Celia in my arms like that anytime I wanted. It was memories of making her laugh and the look in her eyes when she told me her secrets.

"Eli," I say slowly.

"Yeah?" Elijah's watching me with unrestrained glee. His dark hair and eyes are lit with mirth and I have this horrible sinking sensation that he knows everything already.

Or maybe that he knows more than I do.

I swallow and clear my throat. "I hooked up with Celia."

His eyes widen but it's not with surprise so much as...delight.

"Thank God." He drops his head backwards like this is the biggest relief and not a catastrophe.

"I'm being serious here, man," I say. I need clarity. I need help

Hell, I'll take any advice I can get, even if it's from my friend who's never once been in a real relationship.

But Elijah ignores me, still grinning like this is the best news ever.

Personally, I'm pretty sure it's a catastrophe, especially considering the way Celia got all teary-eyed just now.

Why was she crying? I rub a hand over my chest as I follow Elijah out of the elevator. Had I made her cry? Should I have said something about last night? Should we have talked?

Elijah's been talking but I'm not paying attention. At least, not until he says, "...it's about time."

I stop in the middle of the hallway. "What's that supposed to mean?"

Elijah turns back to me, and his expression is patronizing.

Elijah, the biggest player I know. The guy best known for throwing parties and casual hookups, not to mention organizing scavenger hunts—and he's looking at me like I'm a cute little child who's just learned how to add.

"Dude," he says with a shake of his head.

"Don't 'dude' me," I say. "What are you not saying?"

He turns to face straight ahead. He's not talking, but I see his smirk.

I stop short. "Wait, did you...did you *know*?"

He glances back at me and his innocent look is beyond suspicious.

"Did you know she had a thing for me?" I ask.

He grins but keeps on walking.

I chase after him. "How long?" I ask. "And who else knows?"

He holds his hand up and ticks off two fingers. "Uh, *forever*? And everyone."

I stop short again and he continues on, but I hear his laughter drifting down the hallway. "What the...? Seriously?"

Before he can answer, a door opens at the end of the hallway, and Pamela steps out. Behind her, a guy walks out of the room.

Dominic. He's a big guy, impossible to miss. Coach was psyched to recruit him to our team. I think I heard some rumor that he and his twin sister are related to some celebrity or a politician or something? Not that it's important, but these are the random thoughts trying to form in my head as they turn and spot us.

Everyone freezes. Even Elijah, who's watching me with a wary look.

Elijah's not on the basketball team, but he and Ryan have been my best friends for so long now that they know just how much the team means to me. I might not be its brightest star, but the team has given me a place to belong. A place to feel like maybe I add some value. The team has given me a sense of family...and I sure as hell don't want to lose that because Pamela's gotten bored and is looking for attention again.

I stretch my neck and lower my shoulders, giving Elijah a glance to tell him I'm not about to go off the rails. As if I would. He knows I'm not the angry type. And right now I can't even muster much more than irritation at the sight of my ex and her new guy.

Elijah falls into step beside me as we draw close and I see Pamela's eyes narrow into slits. She's ready for a fight.

No, that's not quite right.

I see the way she straightens. The way she picks up her pace and lifts her chin.

She's *looking forward* to a fight.

I let out an exhale that leaves me somehow even more exhausted than I was a second ago. I'm not just tired, I'm freakin' weary.

I feel like my emotions have been put through the wringer these past twenty-four hours as everything I thought I knew was flipped upside down and everything I thought I understood was put to the test.

My realizations from the night before are still ringing in my head as I reach Pamela. I don't want to be my parents.

I won't.

Given half a chance, she'll turn this into a shouting match right here in the hallway, so I speak before she has the chance. "I'm not doing this anymore, Pamela."

Her eyes widen. "What?" she snaps. "What does that even mean?"

The confusion in her eyes is genuine. I just went off script and she's genuinely thrown. All at once I'm hit with a wave of pity. She's just as much a victim here as I am. We're both the bad guys and we're both the victims. But if one of us doesn't walk away for good...

Well, I know how that turns out.

"Pamela, listen to me," I say, all too aware that Dominic has slowed his pace to give us a moment and that Elijah is watching us like he might have to intervene.

Pamela gives an exasperated huff that I know well. "What do you want?"

"I don't want to fight," I say. "I'm not angry that you moved on. In fact, I'm grateful."

"You're—you're *what*?" She looks so offended, like I just slapped her across the face.

I wince because...crap. I'm trying not to hurt her, but it seems that's all I'm capable of.

I clear my throat and glance around, catching Dominic's serious gaze as he slowly heads toward us. I don't care if he hears, since this is for him too, so I say, "I just want you to be happy, Pamela."

She blinks like this is shocking news.

Hell, maybe it is for her. We've been at odds for so long, I'm not sure whether we could ever even be friends.

Yet we didn't see that as a reason that maybe we shouldn't be a couple?

I shake my head, frustrated with myself for letting it get so bad and for allowing it to go on for so long.

"I mean it, Pamela. I want you to be happy, and we both know I'm not that guy."

Her eyes widen and her lips part. I feel like I'm hurting her feelings, and that just sucks because I don't want to do that. I really don't.

I start to back away. "I just want you to be happy," I say again.

"Is this because of Celia?" Her voice is loud and it stops me short in the hallway.

Elijah hisses and even Dominic winces, though I have no idea how much he knows or what he thinks of all this. Does he actually like Pamela?

I hope so.

For her sake, I hope so.

I don't play dumb, but I'm not about to let Celia get dragged into Pamela's need for drama. "No," I say. "This has nothing to do with Celia."

Her lips curve up in a sneer. "I heard about you two spending the night together."

"We were stranded," I say. "It wasn't like that."

Pamela's laugh is loud, harsh, and bitter.

A door clicks open at the end of the hall. Great. Now we're putting on a performance for strangers too.

"Really?" she shoots back. "Because everyone knows that Celia has a thing for you, so are you honestly saying—"

"Nothing happened, Pamela," I say, a little louder than intended. "Celia has nothing to do with this."

"So you're not into her now?" she asks.

"No," I say. Because if I don't, she'll latch onto that suspicion and will use it to feed a fight that I don't want.

It's none of her business how I feel about Celia, just like it's none of my business how she feels about Dominic.

We've been dead in the water for ages now, even if we were still a couple.

Pamela's eyes narrow, and I see it. The jealousy that's always fueled her. Not for the first time, I find myself thinking that she doesn't want me—she just doesn't want anyone else to have me.

I know it's the truth. She likes to think that I'm hers. Maybe she needs that for whatever reason.

"Look..." I move forward and drop my voice. "Celia has nothing to do with this. This is about me and you." I glance over her shoulder at Dominic. "If you've found someone who makes you happy, go for it."

Her face pales.

She expected me to be disappointed, at least. Angry too, no doubt.

"Don't mess up a good thing just to hurt me," I say so quietly no one else can hear. "I'm not worth it."

I don't give her a chance to respond because I'm already turning away, and I hear Dominic say something in a low voice before they step onto the elevator. I let out a sigh and head down the hallway toward—

Celia?

I stop short.

Celia and Noelle are standing at the far end of the hall staring at me, and Celia's face gives nothing away. But Noelle?

She's glaring at me and I know that they heard us talking about Celia. Or at least, they heard Pamela say that everyone knows she has a thing for me.

They likely heard me say that there's nothing between us.

"Shit." Elijah mutters it under his breath.

I flinch. My thoughts exactly.

Noelle takes Celia by the arm and they hurry past us, Noelle mumbling something about how they're in a hurry to get to the presentations.

Celia's expression is blank, and much as I want to stop her, I don't.

She has a presentation to give. I watch her walk away, back straight in the little short-sleeved black dress she borrowed from Noelle. She'd only left to change a little while ago, but somehow she looks perfect. Her hair is blown straight, her lips are pink and she's the picture of a put-together, classy young woman who has plans for her life.

Plans that don't include me. Or any guy, for that matter.

"Good luck," I call after her again just like I had down in the lobby.

She doesn't turn around and my shout seems to hang in the air as the elevator doors close behind her.

I am officially pathetic.

Elijah claps me on the shoulder again, this time in clear sympathy. "Give her time, man. And then go talk to her."

I nod, even though I'm well aware I'm getting advice from a guy who has even less experience with healthy relationships than I do.

Do I talk to her or do I just let her go?

I have no clue, but the thought of letting her go has my insides getting all tight and constricted.

A deep voice calls my name and Elijah and I both turn in surprise to see Dominic didn't get on the elevator with Pamela. Apparently he'd been hanging around, waiting for Celia and Noelle to leave because now he's striding toward us—all six-feet-something of him—and he doesn't stop until he's close.

"I just, uh..." He looks away, looking visibly uncomfortable. "I just wanted to say I'm sorry. I didn't know..." He flinches. "I didn't find out she was with someone until after..."

He winces, and I don't blame him. It's not exactly fun for me either, standing here listening to a near stranger tell me that my ex cheated on me with him.

"I really don't need the details," I say.

"Right." He clears his throat. "But I wanted to apologize. I know we're going to be on the same team and I take that seriously. If I'd known..." He inhales audibly. "I never meant to cause problems. That's...not who I am."

I nod slowly. I couldn't scrounge up jealousy before and I definitely can't now. "You didn't know, man," I say, sticking out a hand to shake his. "It's all good."

We shake and he walks away.

"I actually feel sorry for that guy," Elijah says after a beat.

I let out a huff of amusement. "Yeah. I do too."

"I bet he had no idea what he was getting into," Elijah says with a shake of his head.

I laugh but my stomach sinks. Dominic might not have known what he was getting into with Pamela, but I did. Every time. For years now I've made every wrong choice and I didn't just hurt myself in the process.

I hurt Pamela too.

Sure, it was mutual, but does that get me off the hook? No.

And does it give me the right to try again with a girl who deserves a million times better?

Something inside me plummets because... "Absolutely not."

"Absolutely not, what?" Elijah asks as he pulls out a key card and lets us into the room we're supposed to share.

I shake my head. "Just thinking, that's all."

Elijah arches a brow as he looks over at me. "About how you're gonna make this right with Celia?"

I nod. I will make this right for her. I owe her an apology and an explanation, at the very least.

Elijah laughs. "Good man. It's about time you saw what was right in front of your—Wait. Hold up." His smile fades as he studies me. "Why do you look like someone just offed your dog?"

I don't really care to explain. Not when Elijah's all happy believing me and Celia might be a thing. "Do you ever think maybe you're too screwed up for a real relationship?" I ask instead.

Elijah's not offended. Far from it. He scoffs. "Man, I know I am."

I nod again. "Yeah. I'm starting to realize I'm not that kind of guy either."

Or at least, I'm not yet.

Because Pamela has her faults, but it's time I accept responsibility for how messed up we were. Our friends always joke that Pamela and I are a toxic mix, but maybe it's more than that.

Maybe I'm toxic.

Maybe the best thing I could do for Celia is let her walk away.

I flinch as I think it, my chest tightening in pain like I just jabbed a knife into myself.

I don't want her to go back to being wary around me, and I can't handle her hating me forever. I want...

Ah hell, I don't know what I want.

But I need to do this right. Celia deserves that much.

If I learned anything from Pamela it's that I need to be better at talking. At telling someone how I feel.

The very thought has my throat constricting, but I head

toward the closet where Elijah's hung up some dress shirts. "Can I borrow something?"

"Of course," Elijah says. "What do you need?"

I take a deep breath and let it out slowly. "What are you supposed to wear to these presentations?"

THIRTEEN

Celia

ALL THAT MATTERS is my speech.

I fidget with the cards on my lap and try not to tug at the neckline of this borrowed dress. It's a nice dress. It looks so lovely on Noelle. But without the curves to hold it up, it's dangerously close to sliding off my shoulders.

I close my eyes and say a silent prayer to protect me from any major wardrobe malfunctions during my presentation.

I'm in the hallway waiting for my turn, and I am definitely not thinking about anything other than the most important moment of my life.

I tap the cards to my knee. The hallway is mostly empty except for other presenters who are doing the same thing I am—waiting for their turn. There's an audience full of people in there. Mostly friends, teachers, and, of course, the judges.

And the VIP attendees like, oh, you know—the dean of Cornell's business school.

I draw in a shaky breath. This is it. The moment I've been building toward. I'm definitely not going to screw it up by obsessing over a boy.

Not even if it's *the* boy.

Not even if that boy happened to have kissed me the day before.

And definitely not because I'd overheard him tell his girlfriend-as-of-yesterday-morning that there was nothing going on between us.

Nope. There's no reason to think about that right now.

Because there *isn't* anything going on between us.

"Celia, are you sure you don't want to talk?" Noelle asks.

It's only then I realize I'm currently blowing air out through an imaginary straw and no doubt looking like a freak as I do so.

I shake my head. "Not right now."

Noelle nods, but she doesn't look convinced. She's been asking that for ages now and I'm even less inclined to talk now than I was while blow drying my hair in our hotel room, but something tells me she's not going to stop.

Mara's not either when we eventually connect. Or Addie, when she gets back from her latest trip to see her father.

And it's not like I can blame them. If the situation were reversed and one of them just spent the night alone with the boy they'd been crushing on for a lifetime, I would probably hogtie them to a chair until they spilled every last detail.

So yes. I get it.

And truthfully, I'd been looking forward to getting some

perspective...but that was before the whole Pamela and Heath run-in.

Not that I'm angry.

I'm not.

I'm not even hurt because Heath wasn't lying when he said there was nothing between us. He was basically just confirming what I already knew.

No, I guess the worst thing was the embarrassment.

I was used to my friends knowing my feelings. And if I really thought about it, I probably would have guessed that Elijah and Ryan suspected too. I considered them both friends, and I'm well aware that I acted one way around them when Heath wasn't around and entirely different when he was nearby.

They'd have had to be totally clueless not to at least guess that maybe there was something up there. But to hear Pamela say that she knew. That *everyone* knows...

I wriggle in my seat as I try to shut off the thoughts.

"Celia," Noelle starts, her brow creased with worry. "Are you sure—"

"I can't talk about it now, okay?" I interrupt with a hushed voice, holding the cards up like evidence. "Later. Later I can talk about it."

But I'm already wincing at the thought of telling her, Addie, and Mara about my crazy hot kiss with Heath. Because I know them, and they'll be excited.

Worse, they'll be optimistic.

I might be an optimistic romantic when it comes to others, but I can't be like that for myself. Even if there could be hope, I don't want it.

But they won't get that.

They'll try to talk me into believing in some fantasy that I'd decided long ago I don't actually want.

My heart does this kicking motion and my belly erupts into butterflies like it's trying to protest. Okay fine. Maybe my body wants it. And yeah, okay, my heart too. But they're not in control here and they never will be.

"Miss Kennedy?" A tall, balding man pokes his head out into the hallway and gives me a kind smile. "We're ready for you."

I plaster on a smile of my own and Noelle squeezes my hand as I walk past. "Break a leg."

The walk up to the podium is the longest of my life. I have to blink for my eyes to adjust to the bright lights aimed at me when I get there. Soon enough, I can see.

But I wish I couldn't.

Because now I see the judges with pen and paper, and I see the dean, and the other competitors, and—

Heath?

I blink in surprise a few times as I focus on him. Yeah, that's him all right. He's lounging back in his seat, wearing a new shirt and freshly shaved, and with a grin that absolutely steals my heart.

I swear I can feel it leave my body like he just stole it out from underneath me.

He came.

Heath came to my presentation. I can't even comprehend this right now because aside from Noelle who's claiming a spot in the back, none of the other club members are here. And I don't blame them. We've all heard each other's presentations countless times and there's a huge city out there just waiting to be explored.

"Whenever you're ready, Miss Kennedy," the same balding man says as he takes a seat in the front row.

I decide to focus on him. He's got a kind smile and a

hopeful arch to his eyebrows like he can't wait for me to wow him.

I'll do my best, sir.

I clear my throat, give my best smile, and dive in.

I do well, if I do say so myself. I mean, I'm not about to win any awards for oration or anything, but I manage to make it through without my voice shaking or sweat dripping down my face, so I'm calling it a win.

"...and if you have any questions, I'd be happy to answer," I finish, taking a deep breath now that it's over.

The faces that greet me are smiling, and the judges are jotting down notes. I shouldn't look at Heath. I am not here seeking his approval, dang it. So, nope. Not going to look over at—

Oh crap, I looked.

I looked, and he's...smiling. Sort of. But there's something wrong. It's in the tightness around his eyes. The way he's peering at me like he's waiting for me to catch on or read his mind or—

My lips part on a squeak as it clicks. I forgot the part about sustainability.

Again.

I just barely refrain from slapping a palm to my forehead because—that's the most important part! How could I forget it?

Crap, crap, crap. My breathing is coming faster. How weird would it look if I were to breathe out through a straw right now?

I messed up. My big opportunity to wow the dean and I messed it up. Maybe it's not too late. I'm scrambling to come up with a way to tell the judges that I completely flaked on my speech and that I'd like to do it again, but then...

A hand shoots up.

Heath's hand. He's waving it in the air like he's waiting to be called on.

"Um..." I look around but the judges are still scribbling. I'm pretty sure the questions typically come from the judges but no one interrupts to stop me, so I turn to Heath in confusion. "Yes?"

"I was just wondering," he says slowly, his brows drawn together in a thoughtful expression. "How sustainable is this new product?"

I grin, a wave of gratitude rushing over me with such strength I feel like I might topple over. Instead, I straighten. "Great question," I say, getting a cute little smirk in return from Heath.

I turn to face the judges as I launch into the sustainability section as though I'm honestly just coming up with this on the fly.

My chest swells with excitement as I see all the heads nodding, all the eyes on me paying attention once more, all the expressions brightening with approval.

I'm totally ready to faint by the time the questions are over. I'm having a hard time breathing, but not out of panic.

This is sheer excitement because...I did it.

I totally nailed it.

I'm barely out in the hallway when Noelle races out and pounces on me with a shout. "You kicked butt, lady!"

I'm laughing as she dances me around like I'm a puppet, but we both stop short when Heath walks out, a smile stretching from ear to ear. He gets close and stops. "You did it."

I smile. Not even the sight of Heath Reilly can burst this bubble. Or, maybe him being here is making the bubble ten times bigger?

Crap.

"Great job, Cece," he says with that sweet smile that makes my heart throb like it's wounded.

"Cece?" Noelle laughs. "What am I missing here? One day together and you two have nicknames for each other?"

I know she's dying to ask more questions—*real* questions. But awesome friend that she is, she refrains. She does a stellar job of keeping this little exchange tension free instead, filling the silence with laughter and jokes and chit-chat.

It's exactly *unlike* the awkward moment when Noelle and I overheard him and Pamela talking about me.

Me and my infamous crush.

My stomach churns. Is the earth opening up to swallow me whole or is that just my imagination?

"We need to go out and celebrate," Noelle says, loudly and exuberantly talking over any tense silence on my end.

"Yes," I manage to say. "Definitely."

Noelle looks to Heath, who nods quickly. "Yeah, of course. Celia deserves to be celebrated."

I can feel my cheeks catching fire because he's giving me this affectionate smile like he's proud of me or something.

"Everyone should be celebrated," I say quickly. "We all worked hard and performed well."

He looks like he's trying not to laugh and I realize my mistake.

"Except for you," I say, tempering it with a smile that makes him laugh. "You didn't give your presentation."

"I did not," he agrees easily. "But something tells me our group was better off for not having me and Pamela on the same team."

I swear, the mention of Pamela's name is a record-scratcher out here in the hall. I hold my breath, and not even

Noelle is smooth enough to cover this sudden and intense wave of humiliation as I'm suddenly back in that hallway listening to him say loudly and clearly that he is not into me.

I suck in a quick breath and Heath's gaze lands on me, the laughter gone now, but a small smile still in place. He catches my eye and nods toward a little alcove. "Can I talk to you for one sec?"

My stomach plummets, but there's only one answer to give. "Of course."

Of course I'll have a private moment with you.

Of course I'll nod while you explain away that awkward moment.

Of course I'll smile and agree that last night was a mistake. That we should just be friends.

It's for the best, I tell myself as I follow just behind him, resisting the urge to sneak a look in Noelle's direction for support.

"What's up?" I say when we come to a stop.

He glances toward the auditorium. "You were really great in there. Really," he says again. "Really great."

I see his throat work as he swallows.

He's nervous. The king of brooding is actually nervous. This is so at odds with the laid back guy I've always known that I'm not sure what to make of it. I've never seen him so tense or so uncomfortable around anyone. I'm usually the one who gets all awkward and weird, but now—

I blink in horror. Oh God. I've broken Heath Reily.

"I know you heard me and Pamela talking," he starts.

My heart kicks into high gear as humiliation crashes over me and disappointment nearly drowns me. *Oh God, Oh God, please just let me get through this without embarrassing myself any further.*

"It's fine," I say quickly in a high, tight voice and with a wave of my hand.

"I was just saying what I had to to put an end to the conversation," he continues, even though it's clearly killing both of us.

"Fine," I mutter, somewhat desperately. "It's totally fine."

Please stop talking. I can't take the sympathy and regret I see in his eyes. I can't stand the pity that has his gorgeous hazel eyes all crinkled up at the corners

I know this look. This is the look every guy has given a girl before he tells her he only thinks of her as a friend.

He shoves his hands in his pockets. "I didn't want you to think—"

"I don't," I say quickly. Too quickly if his rapid blinking is anything to go by.

He frowns. "It looked like maybe you were upset—"

"I wasn't," I say.

He blinks again. "Okay, but I do think you and I should—"

"We will." I say this with a bright smile even though I have no idea what I've just agreed to. You and I should...what? What was he going to say?

It's too late to ask now, though. And besides, the door is swinging open and Mr. Deckman is striding toward me with open arms. "She came and she conquered!"

I laugh because it's expected. Mr. Deckman calls me over and it takes everything in me not to run away from Heath.

I walk over at a totally normal pace...I think.

"I talked to Dean Gladwell," Mr. Deckman says. "She was blown away by your proposal."

"Really?" My voice is convincingly enthusiastic, and my smile stretches so far it hurts my cheeks.

Of course it does. This is what I wanted.

"That's amazing," Noelle says from behind me.

Mr. Deckman was talking loudly enough for everyone in the hallway to hear.

"Yeah, that's great news," Heath says.

His voice is so close that I jump.

I turn to find him staring at me like he's seeing me for the first time.

Noelle puts a hand on his arm and says something to him I can't hear. Then she smiles at me. "We'll let you guys talk," she says. "See you back at the room?"

I nod. "I'll catch up with you guys later."

I turn back to Mr. Deckman, determined to give him my full attention.

After all, this is everything I wanted.

But no matter how much I try and focus, I'm still keenly aware of the sound of Heath's footsteps walking away.

This presentation and the potential interview...it's all that matters.

But as much as I tell myself that, it doesn't change the fact that when Heath's footsteps fade to nothing, my heart feels like it's falling apart.

FOURTEEN

Heath

WELL. That went...

Badly.

It went badly.

I run a hand over my hair and let out a loud exhale. Why sugarcoat the truth?

"So, you want to tell me what's going on with you two?" Noelle is standing at my side and staring down the hallway where we'd left Celia.

Or rather, where we'd both watched her run away from me.

Fine. Maybe she was called away, but I swear I haven't seen a girl so eager to escape a situation since the last *Saw* movie.

Noelle turns to face me as we step into the elevator and she hits the button for our floor. "Well?"

I eye her for a long moment as I consider. It's not that I don't trust Noelle. I do. We've been friends for years, but she's much closer to Celia and I don't want to put her in the middle.

But, at the same time, I'm dying to get some answers here. I'd kill for some insights on how to make things right with Celia. Because that attempt back there?

I'm pretty sure that was a massive fail.

Noelle arches a brow, clearly annoyed at being kept waiting.

"How much did she tell you?" I hedge.

She rolls her eyes. "Everything. Obviously."

I let out a loud exhale as I fall back against the wall. "Does she hate me for kissing her?"

Noelle stares at me wide-eyed and I turn my gaze to look at the numbers as we climb higher.

I'll admit it. I'd kinda shocked myself with that question. But I had to know, because Celia's reaction to me just now...

I mean, I'd thought she hated me before. But that was *before*. I thought things were different now that—

"You *kissed* her?" Noelle's voice is so loud next to me that I jerk away from the wall with a start.

"What?" I turn to see her gaping at me in shock.

Crap. She hadn't known about the kiss.

"But you said...You said..." I jab a finger in her direction. "You said she told you everything."

She doesn't even flinch. "I lied."

"You—" I can't even finish because I'm too busy staring at her in disbelief.

"What I meant was, she *will* tell me everything...*eventually*." She meets my gaze and shrugs. "What? She didn't have time to tell me, but you do." She crosses her arms. "So spill."

I throw my hands out, still gaping at the nerve of this girl. "*Noelle,*" I say.

She arches her brows and says my name with the same inflection. "*Heath.*"

When I don't immediately respond, she sighs. "Look, you and I both know that confronting emotions is not exactly Celia's strong suit." She pinches her lips before adding, "Especially when it comes to you."

I frown. She has a point. Celia has proven to be exceptionally clever at avoiding me. I flinch because... "She's not going to do that again, is she? Just...pretend I don't exist?"

Noelle arches her brows. "I don't know. Why don't you tell me what went down between you two and I'll tell you how I think she'll handle it."

We face one another in a silent standoff until the elevator dings and the door opens. I gesture for her to go first. "Sorry, Noelle. Much as I'd love your help, I don't think it's my place to share her story."

Noelle's sigh is dramatic. "I hate it that you're right." She flashes me a sudden and impish grin. "I guess I'll just have to wait for her to get done with Mr. Deckman so I can pry it out of her instead."

I nod, but my insides are falling flat because I'm no closer to knowing how to handle this than I had been two minutes ago.

"Look..." Noelle stops short in the hallway and turns to me. "From what little I do know, I'd say you owe her an explanation for what went on in the hallway between you and Pamela today."

I nod quickly. "That's what I was trying to do just now but she barely let me get a word in edgewise."

Noelle's stare is alarmingly direct. "Do you like her?"

I open my mouth and shut it again. Not because I don't know the answer. But because I do.

I like Celia Kennedy.

A lot.

I like her so much it scares the crap out of me. I like her more than I've ever liked any girl, even Pamela back when we first got together.

I like her in a way that makes me want to change. To try. To become a guy who's worthy of her.

I swallow hard because the thoughts are hitting me like a sucker punch.

Holy crap. I like this girl so much it's terrifying. Because she's made it clear that she doesn't want anything with any guy. Not now, at least.

And because she liked me before she really knew me, and I'm more than a little worried that the more she gets to know me the more she'll see that she was wrong about me.

But the scariest part is that I like her so much, I want to protect her from anyone who could hurt her. Which means, I might very well need to protect her from *me*.

This last run-in with Pamela was a great reminder that even when I had good intentions, all I ever did was hurt that girl.

Would it be any different with Celia if she gave me a chance?

Maybe. I'd like to think so. But what if it's not? What if the problem wasn't Pamela, or the two of us together, but *me*? What if *I'm* too messed up for a real, healthy, normal relationship?

"Whoa," Noelle says slowly, her voice low and wary. "I don't know what's going on in that pretty head of yours, but I think it's safe to say you need to chill."

I blink because I'd sort of forgotten that Noelle was

even here as I'd gone down that hole of Celia-related terrors. I take a deep breath and look away. "I need to talk to her."

"Yeah, you do," she says. "If you kissed her, then you like her—"

I go to interrupt but she holds up a hand. "Cut the crap, Heath. I've known you for way too long. You're not some jerk who's only out to get laid. Besides, one look at the way you were acting around Celia earlier and it's obvious that you care."

I blink again because...was it so obvious?

"You two are killing me," Noelle mutters, but she's wearing a little smile that makes it sound almost affectionate. She steps toward me and grabs me by my shoulders. "Man up and talk to her already."

She starts to walk away and I hurry to catch up. "I don't think she wants to talk to me."

"Ya think?" She starts to laugh. When she glances over and sees I'm most definitely not laughing, she sighs. "If you haven't noticed yet, our girl only freaks around one particular guy and for one particular reason." She glances over at me again. "I don't doubt that she doesn't want to talk to you, but that's exactly why you two need to talk. Get it?"

I stop in front of the room I share with Elijah, and she keeps walking toward hers.

She turns back with a wink. "If you haven't figured that out yet, you're not as smart as I thought you were."

My heart starts to pound heavily, this time with excitement or anticipation or...hope.

"Wait."

She stops and arches her brows, waiting for me to speak.

I have more questions popping up than I can handle so I

end up making a statement. "She doesn't want a relationship."

Noelle nods slowly. "Then I guess you've got your work cut out for you."

She flashes me a brilliant grin before disappearing into her room and I slide out my key card for mine.

"Finally," Elijah says as I enter. "You ready to check out the big city or what?"

"Ready as I'll ever be," I say.

"Don't worry, man," Elijah says. "Celia will be there. You two will work this out."

I nod. He seems so confident. Noelle too. And once again I'm hit with this annoying sensation that my friends know more about my life than I do.

"What?" Elijah asks. "What's with that look?"

I shrug. "I don't know what to say to her," I admit. "And even if I did, I don't know if I should."

He nods slowly and then winces with regret. "Honestly, man, it's Ryan you should be talking to, not me."

I chuckle. "I know." Ryan's the only one of us in a functional, loving, committed relationship. "But he's not here." I arch my brows in a prompt.

He might not have great advice, but right now I'll take all the help I can get.

Elijah sighs. "Fine. If you want to know what I think, it's this—you take everything so seriously." He nodded toward the hallway. "You and Celia both do. She's too driven and worried about what comes next, and you're too caught up in your own head thanks to your ex and her mind games."

I stare at Elijah for a long beat. "Don't hold back," I say mildly. "Tell me how you really feel."

Elijah laughs and holds his hands up in defense. "Hey, man, you asked."

I shake my head with a rueful chuckle. "Yeah, I guess I did. So, let's say you're right, and she and I are taking this all way too seriously. What's your big advice?"

Elijah laughs as he walks past me toward the door. "I thought it was obvious." He glances back at me with a devilish grin. "Show the girl a good time."

FIFTEEN

Celia

I TUG at the sweater dress Noelle insisted I try on. "If this barely covers my thighs, how on earth does this fit you?" I ask.

I'm one hundred percent serious, but Noelle just laughs.

This dress is the exact opposite of the one I'd just worn to the presentation. Where that had been demure, and understated, and way more in keeping with my preppy style, this was...not.

It was a soft, cream, knitted number that clung to every curve. It was stretchy, which I presumed was how it managed to fit me so snugly even though I didn't have Noelle's height or curves.

Noelle stands behind me in the mirror. "You look hot," she declares.

"Let me see!" Mara's voice shouts at us from the bed.

Noelle reaches for the phone where she has Mara on

video chat and holds it up to face me. I turn and do some ridiculous poses that make all three of us crack up.

"Yaass," Mara shouts. "You get it, girl."

Noelle's laughing, but I see her gaze sharpen on me and I know my brief respite from questions is about to run out.

"Actually, our girl here's already getting it. Isn't that right, *Cece*?"

I roll my eyes, my cheeks flaming at the mention of that nickname. "I don't know what you think you know," I start.

"Don't even try it, sweetcheeks," Noelle says, reaching out to pat my cheek condescendingly. "I already know you two kissed."

"*What?*" Mara's voice is a screech that makes me and Noelle both wince. "Did I hear her right?" she demands. Then her voice gets muffled for a bit. After a second, she comes back on. "Sorry. Apparently I was a little too loud so my mom and Ryan came running in here because they thought there was an intruder."

She muffles the phone again but Noelle and I exchange a look when we hear her tell them, "Celia and Heath. No, I'm not kidding. I'm totally serious. Hang on." Then to us, "Celia, my mom is begging me to remind you to use protection."

Noelle bursts out in a cackle as I choke and sputter with protests.

Mara's talking to someone in the background again. We both hear her laugh before returning to talk to us. "Okay, and Ryan's trying to claim that he knew this was going to happen."

"I totally called it too," Noelle says. "I mean as soon as I heard that Pamela had ended things again, I knew this was Celia's time."

My time?

Please. That makes it sound like fate, or something, and not the bizarre series of unfortunate disasters that made up our travel day.

I shake my head in disbelief, making a beeline for the bathroom where I help myself to Noelle's makeup. Not ones to be ignored, however, Noelle follows me in there and Mara swears up and down that she's alone again and anything I tell her will stay between the three of us.

"I wish Addie was around," Noelle says with a frown. "I wonder why she didn't pick up."

"You know how crazy she gets when she goes to stay at her dad's with the new stepfamily," Mara says. "But she's gonna be so bummed she missed this."

Truthfully, I wish Addie was here too. Mainly because I miss my kindhearted, gentle little redheaded friend, but also because she'd be the quiet, sweet voice of reason right now. As opposed to—

"I swear, Celia, if you do not spill every single detail, I'm gonna call Cornell and tell them that you cheated on the SATs," Noelle says.

Mara laughs. "She'll do it, too. Come on, Celia. Don't make us wear you down."

And they will. I meet my own reflection and sigh. Fine. Whatever. It's not like I could avoid this forever. "Okay, so it all started when we both missed the first train…"

A little while later they were all caught up and I was a knit-clad ball of confusion.

"I still don't get what the problem is," Mara says, her voice still high with excitement. "He kissed you. *He* kissed *you.*"

I flinch because it's the one phrase she hasn't stopped repeating since I said it.

I just hope she's done with the squealing and cheering

because our neighbors in this hotel have got to be getting annoyed with that.

"I don't see the problem either," Noelle says. She sounds less excited and more...annoyed. "He likes you, Celia. Anyone can see that."

"Since when?" I shoot back. "What everyone can see is that Heath's a nice guy. He might've liked kissing me, but that's not the same thing as liking me."

Noelle addresses her next comment to Mara. "She's still pissed because we caught him having one of his tiffs with Pamela."

"Ahh," Mara says. "You don't think they're getting back together, do you?"

"Sounds like Pamela's already moved on," Noelle says. "But you know how that goes."

Yes. We all knew very well how this typically went. Pamela hooks up with someone and throws it in his face. Heath gets mad. They break up. They fight. They get back together. They fight again.

It's always some variation of the same pattern.

And while I want to make a joke about it, while I want to wave it away with a roll of my eyes—I can't. Because I can still vividly remember the look in Heath's eyes when he turned to face me and said, *I don't want to be my parents either*.

Suddenly brushing off his toxic relationship with Pamela just feels wrong. Like making light of a tragedy.

"Well, Celia, what did Heath say when you asked him about it?" Mara asks.

"Um..." I shoot Noelle a guilty glance.

Noelle snorts. "She didn't talk to him about it."

Mara's sigh fills the bathroom, and I hurry into action, tidying up the hair brushes and makeup that's lying around.

"Celia," Mara says in a decidedly motherly tone.

Honestly, who needs an involved mother when one had Mara and her mother to fill in?

I ignore her.

"You have to talk to him," she continues. "Give him a chance to explain."

"That's what *I* said." Noelle arches her brows in smug triumph.

"Why?" I turn to face Noelle and the phone she's still holding.

"Because," Mara says. "What if he likes you?"

"He doesn't know me," I say.

"What if he wants to get to know you?" Noelle shoots back.

I clamp my mouth shut. But then the silence draws out too long so I shrug. "I don't know."

Silence again. And then Mara breaks it with a too-gentle voice that inexplicably makes me want to cry. "Is this because of your whole not-gonna-date pact you made when you were six?"

I wrinkle my nose. She makes it sound so...juvenile. "It's a good plan."

Noelle's expression isn't unkind, but she's clearly not convinced.

"Uh huh." Mara's clearly not either.

Silence falls as I fidget with the brush in my hands.

"You know," Mara continues slowly. "Sometimes plans change as we get older."

"Especially plans made when we were six," Noelle adds. "I mean, I planned to live in Disneyworld and be a full-time princess when I was six."

I choke on a laugh and Mara snickers on her end of the line.

"But things change," Noelle says.

I turn away. "Yeah, well. I'm not sure I want to change this plan."

Noelle tries again. "But if he likes you—"

"That's a big if," I say.

"If he *does*, don't you deserve to know that?" she continues. "And don't you think, either way, he deserves to know how you feel as well?"

I stare at her because...dang it. I hate that she's right.

"And for what it's worth, Celia," Mara says on her end. "Even if it turns out this crush is mutual, that doesn't necessarily mean it's going to be some life-altering relationship that lasts forever and ever."

I purse my lips and look away. Of course I know that.

"It might not be serious on either side once you get to know each other better," she continues, clearly warming to her topic. "For all you know, your feelings for him might fade the more you get to know him."

I bite my lip as I consider that. Doubtful, considering the fact that the more I've gotten to know him, the more I've found to like. But I see her point, and it has merit.

Mara's voice cuts into my thoughts again. "Or, vice versa," she says. "He could get to know you better and realize it was just a one-night thing."

I frown. "Not helping," I mutter.

"Or..." Noelle draws the word out meaningfully. "It could just be..." She leans in and lowers her voice. "Fun! Gasp!" She actually gasps the word *gasp* which makes me giggle and Mara burst out in a laugh.

"She's right, you know," Mara says. "If nothing else, you owe it to yourself to get to know him better and see if you actually like him. A crush from afar is totally different from having feelings for someone you're intimately acquainted with." She pauses and I can see her shrug on the phone's screen. "You might get to know him and decide he's not as great as you thought."

I nod as if I'm considering that, but given what I've learned about him over the past twenty-four hours...I doubt it. I seriously doubt it.

"I'll tell you what," I say as I drag on the same heels I've been wearing since this trip started. Was it seriously only one day ago? "I promise that I'll talk to him." I look to Mara and then Noelle, hoping this will be at least enough to give me some breathing room. "Okay?"

Noelle grins. "Perfect." She holds up her phone. "Because we were supposed to meet Heath and Elijah in the lobby ten minutes ago."

SIXTEEN

Heath

MOST OF THE other students from our school left a while ago. They hadn't been waiting around for the solo presentations to end, and so when Celia steps off the elevator, we spot each other instantly.

Scratch that.

She spots me.

I have the wind knocked out of me by her. My jaw literally drops at the sight of her coming toward me in this figure-hugging dress that makes my mouth go dry and my heart surge into action.

Holy crap, she's hot.

I mean, I knew she was pretty. And yes, cute. And beautiful too.

Okay, fine. Maybe this shouldn't come as a surprise to me at all. But walking toward me right now, the revelation feels like the clouds just parted and the sun's shining down to highlight the fact that Celia Kennedy is hotter than hell.

"Hey, sexy ladies," Elijah shouts out because that's the sort of thing Elijah does.

Noelle gives this sexy pout and starts strutting like she's on the catwalk because that's the sort of thing *she* does.

Celia grins at their antics, but it fades to a shy smile when she glances in my direction and drops her eyes.

Nope. I am not having this. Up until this morning we'd been good. Better than good. We were starting to become friends, at the very least, and if she thinks I'm letting her go back to avoiding me like I'm a walking plague, she'd better think again.

I head toward her and throw an arm around her shoulders as Elijah and Noelle flank us and we head out onto the busy sidewalk.

"Where to first?" Noelle asks.

"Central Park," I say. Because I've done my research. And of the items that Celia listed yesterday, this one is walkable and en route to our second destination.

"Sounds good to me," Noelle says.

"This way." I point north and we find ourselves walking against an oncoming tide of pedestrian traffic so Noelle and Elijah go in front of us.

I look down to see Celia peeking up at me.

"What?" I ask. "Think I don't know how to read a map?" I hold up my phone for evidence.

She smiles. "Just didn't know you were so excited for sightseeing."

"I'm not," I say. "But you are. And this was first on your list."

Her brows hitch up slightly in surprise. "You remember that?"

I remember everything. Every single word out of her

mouth. Every sigh. Every frown. Every shiver and every laugh.

But I'm not sure how to say that without sounding creepy so I just smile and squeeze her shoulders.

She points to my phone. "It's working?"

I grimace. "For now."

She giggles and the sound is so sweet it makes my teeth ache. "Then maybe we should stop at at a phone store or—"

"I don't think so," I say.

"No?"

I give her a rueful grin. "Not unless your mom wouldn't notice an extra cell phone charge on that lovely credit card of hers."

"Oh." She clamps her mouth shut. "Sorry."

I shrug. "Don't be. Like I said, I've done my research. There's plenty we can do on a shoestring budget."

"Oh yeah? Like what?"

Central Park comes into view and I gesture as though I'd just conjured it. "Like this."

Her face lights up and some of my earlier worries melt away. I'm starting to think Elijah has the right idea. I do need to talk to Celia, but not when she's so guarded she might as well be behind locked doors.

Do I like her?

Yes.

Would I be good for her?

That's debatable.

But maybe the fact that I'm terrible at relationships doesn't matter because she's not looking for a boyfriend anyway. So...where does that leave us?

No idea.

"Oh my gosh." She grabs my hand and tugs. "They have horses!"

And we're off, outpacing Noelle and Elijah in Celia's excitement to check out the horse-drawn carriages that, sadly, I can't afford. But Celia doesn't seem to care. She's happy just talking to the drivers and patting the horses' necks. Noelle and I have to drag her away to our next destination.

"The Met?" Celia stops short when she spies the giant museum up ahead. She turns to me with a question in her eyes and I hold up tickets.

"I talked to Mr. Deckman and he worked out a deal with the museum. Some sort of student program they have —*oof*."

Celia's arms wrap around my middle so unexpectedly, I stop short.

"Thank you," she says as she squeezes me.

For a second I hover there awkwardly until I let my arms drop and wrap around her. And then I'm holding her tight, dipping my head until my lips graze the top of her head. "Does this mean you forgive me?" I ask softly.

She stiffens in my arms and I glance around us to see that Noelle and Elijah are laughing up ahead but giving us some space.

Celia pulls back and her cheeks are pink. "There's nothing to forgive—"

"Yes." I take her by the shoulders. "There is. And I need you to let me talk."

She opens her mouth and then clamps it shut with a nod. She doesn't look upset, but I feel her tense under my grip.

"I like you." The words come out on a rush of air and...they're not at all what I meant to say.

"What?" Her eyes are wide as saucers.

"I—" I clear my throat. "I like you, Celia. I like being

around you, I like talking to you, I love hearing what you have to say—"

"I-I—" She stops trying to speak and stares up at me some more.

"I'm not telling you that because I want to try and talk you into something," I say.

My insides start to crumble because…that's a lie. That's exactly what I want to do. But I shouldn't. It's a bad idea for so many reasons.

I hesitate as I stare down into her big brown eyes.

Believe it or not, telling Celia I like her was the easy part. It came out like I'd just been waiting for the chance to say it. But this…? This is the hard part. "I know how you feel about dating. And as for me, I don't think I should rush into anything with anyone either."

I regret the words instantly. Even though I know they make sense, I wish I could pull them back and stuff them back inside.

She blinks. "You don't?"

I swallow hard. She's so close I could lean down and kiss her.

"No. I mean…" I sigh. This sucks. I do like her. I like her a lot. I like her so much that I know I need to do right by her. "I *do* want to see where this could go, but I don't think I should. With my track record, I think maybe I should take some time on my own, you know? Sort through…stuff."

The word *stuff* sounds so ludicrously stupid that I cringe. My words seem to hang there in the air between us as the sounds of childrens' laughter and passing tourists surround us.

"Yeah," she finally says softly. "I get that."

Is that disappointment in her eyes? If it is, it goes away

quickly and she gives me another shy smile. "That's smart," she says. "You should focus on you."

"And *you* should focus on *you*," I add.

There's a finality here that I hate, but the smile she gives me helps. A lot.

"I know you overheard Pamela and me," I say. "And I just want you to know that I wasn't telling the truth."

Her brows hitch up in question.

"There was something between us. Or..." I scrub the back of my neck in discomfort. "Or for me there was at least."

She dips her head, but I hear her soft, "For me too."

And just like that I'm thinking of *maybes* and *one days*. But for now... I reach for her hand. "Come on," I say. "We don't have long until they close."

Celia races along beside me until we catch up to Noelle and Elijah.

"About time," Noelle says.

"You two good?" Elijah asks, his gaze dropping to our linked hands.

I nod and am happy beyond belief to see Celia do the same. Celia's not just good. She's better than good. Celia comes alive in the museum. But it's my response that I'm most amazed by.

I love it here. Like, I freakin' love this place, and I can't even say why.

I get hit with that crazy energy we first experienced when we walked into Grand Central. That feeling like the world is huge and I am small, but in the very best of ways.

It's invigorating. It's humbling. I guess that's how this city makes me feel, in general. But this museum...

"I love it here." I blurt this out so suddenly when we're in the Egyptian room that Celia stops short to stare at me.

"You do?" Anyone else would probably make a joke or say *that's nice*, but Celia tips her head to the side and says, "Why?"

I think of all the crazy, disjointed thoughts flooding my head, and what I settle on is, "I love that this exists." I glance around us and I can feel a goofy smile tugging at my lips. "I love that people worked so hard to make these things and that we're here admiring it all so many years later." That sounds lame, but I try again. "I like that people went to so much trouble to just...say what they had to say."

"To express themselves," she murmurs, nodding in agreement as we head toward the next room. She nods. "Yeah. I love that too."

And then, when we've walked a little further, she adds, "I like that all this was accomplished by everyday people. I mean, some were obviously way more talented than others, but *people* made this stuff."

"They felt *compelled* to make this stuff," I add.

"Exactly," she whispers.

We share a smile that basically eviscerates my insides. It's a smile that says we're on the same page and speaking the same language, even if neither of us is doing an amazing job of putting it into words. We're feeling the same awe and amazement, and that only makes this whole experience that much better.

After the museum, Noelle gets a text from one of her friends and we agree to meet up with a group of our classmates in the Koreatown area for karaoke.

Like before, Noelle and Elijah go ahead of us, laughing and talking, while Celia and I fall behind.

"I love this city," she says. Turning to me with a smile, she adds, "I thought I would like it, but it's so much more than I expected." She bites her lip and looks around us at the towering buildings and throngs of people. "It makes me realize there might be so much more for us, you know? After high school. After Lakeview."

I nod. For her, yes. For me? I don't know. I haven't given the future much thought, but the more time I spend with Celia, the longer we're here together...

Maybe it's this city, or the fact that we're in a strange place without our families, but I feel it too. Like, maybe our lives in Lakeview are a part of the past and like the future is stretched out before us.

It's a good feeling. It's a terrifying feeling. It's excitement and fear and nerves and anticipation all rolled together, and cheesy as it might sound...it makes me feel like I can be anything. Like I can be any*one*.

My heart gives a little tug, because the person I want to be is the person worthy of Celia Kennedy. I glance down to find her smiling, lost in her own thoughts.

I want to be the guy who gets this girl.

"I'm glad you didn't go back to Lakeview," she says quietly, slipping her hand into mine like it's the most natural thing in the world as we merge with other pedestrians heading downtown. She looks up at me and it's impossible to read what she's thinking when she gives me this sweet little smile.

"Me too," I say, squeezing her hand.

Her brows come down, and for a second it looks like she might say more, but she clamps her lips shut instead, turning to face forward as we follow Noelle and Elijah down the block.

Whatever she's thinking about, she's clearly not ready to share. But when she's ready to talk about it, she'll tell me.

I hope.

I glance down at her face, which is upturned as she

checks out the highrises around us. I hope she tells me what she's thinking. I hope one day I'm the guy she tells her secrets to, the person to whom she confides her dreams and her plans and her desires.

I swallow hard because...these thoughts? They're the sort of future I never thought to imagine for myself.

She catches me staring and smiles. "What is it?"

I take a deep breath. "For the first time ever, I actually want to think about what comes next."

Her smile blooms with understanding and my heart stutters like a machine gun in response. I love the fact that she gets this. That she doesn't laugh and doesn't ask questions. She nods like she understands perfectly.

When we reach Koreatown, I look over to see her brilliant smile as she takes in the neon Koreon signs that line each of the buildings. She reaches for my hand and squeezes. "I love this so much."

I grin down at her, my heart swelling in my chest until it's hard to breathe. "Me too."

SEVENTEEN

Celia

THIS MIGHT BE the best day ever.

I mean it. I'm not sure I've ever had more fun or seen such amazing things or had such a fantastic success like I'd had with my presentation.

Life is good.

Life is so freakin' good.

And it just keeps getting better. During our outing, I get a text from Mr. Deckman telling me that the interview with the dean is on for tomorrow afternoon at the hotel. I tell the others and I honestly think Heath might be more excited than I am. He throws his arms up in a cheer that nearly drowns out the awful singing going on by our classmates on stage.

We have to get back to the hotel because we have a curfew, but after Noelle and I say goodnight to the boys, and settle into our own rooms, I'm almost too giddy to sleep.

I aced my presentation, I got the interview of my dreams, and my crush…

I grin up at the ceiling, my heart slamming around in my chest like a pinball.

My crush likes me.

I don't how to feel about this. My heart does a backflip that makes my belly tighten and my lungs hitch.

Okay, that's not true. I know exactly how I feel about this. Hearing him say those words was like a jolt of joy right into my bloodstream.

So yeah, I know how it makes me *feel*.

It's my brain that's having a hard time getting on board. It's pinging back and forth between excitement that my lifelong crush is reciprocated, disappointment because he doesn't want to act on that, and relief because…he doesn't want to act on that.

It's confusing.

Rather than try to sort out the roller coaster of emotions going on inside me, I focus instead on this new side of Heath I'd seen today. I'd thought I'd seen it all after spending so much time together traveling. But watching him light up over art? That was new. And hearing him try to put his feelings into words wasn't just sweet, it was…humbling.

That's the only word I can think of to describe it.

I didn't have to know Heath well to know that he doesn't open up often, and putting his feelings into words like that was rare. It was new. And awesome. And it made me feel absurdly lucky, like I'd won the Heath lottery.

Weird, right?

Yeah. Totally weird.

And it does nothing to help my confusion. I might be

even more confused today than I was after our kiss. But at the very least we're becoming friends, right?

And thinking of him as a friend lets me do what I do best—plan for the future.

Not my future, for once. Mine is good to go now that I have the interview scheduled for tomorrow. But Heath...?

He made it clear back at the motel that he hasn't given college any thought. He hadn't given the future, in general, any thought. But he's starting to think about it, and whether it's weird or not, I want to help him.

Because he's a friend. And that's what friends do. Right?

Luckily the day catches up with me and I drift off to sleep before I can overanalyze any longer. And when I wake up the next morning, I have a plan.

It's clear at breakfast that we're all antsy to get back out there and see more sights. Noelle and Elijah sign up for one of those sightseeing cruises that circle Manhattan, but since that could potentially make me late for my interview, I pass.

Heath bails on that too.

I try not to read into this. I mean, I really try. Didn't we already agree that this was a non-starter? We'd both said quite clearly that it was best if we keep this a platonic friendship.

Had I forgotten that pledge a few times yesterday when he was being so sweet and enthusiastic about art and karaoke? Yes. Of course. Who would not be charmed by his absurdly adorable awkwardness when Noelle and Elijah pulled him up onstage to sing a Michael Jackson song.

But he'd given that sheepish grin and a shrug and gone along with it because...Gah!

Enough. I will not spend my entire day mooning over my crush. I refuse.

"You ready?" Heath asks as the others start to file out of the fast food place where we've grabbed breakfast.

"For what?" I ask.

He makes a show of cracking his knuckles, his mouth set in a smirk. "Oh, I've got plans."

I start to laugh but I'm shaking my head. "I've got plans too, and mine are going to win."

He rests his elbows on the table between us. "Oh yeah? Why's that?"

I answer with a grin and start to laugh when he follows close behind me, hounding me for answers. An idea had been brewing all last night and into this morning. And after a quick chat with Mr. Deckman, it seemed like a no brainer.

"We're going to check out the colleges around town," I inform him.

He stops short and gets an angry glare from a pedestrian who had to walk around him in return. "What?"

"And some galleries in Chelsea, too," I add like I didn't hear his question.

"Why are we checking out colleges?" he asks. "Are you thinking about backup options if Cornell doesn't work out?"

I stare up at him. "No. Of course not. Cornell has always been the plan."

His lips twitch like he's trying not to smile. "Okay then, so why are we checking out college campuses?"

I shrug, turning away. "Why not?"

"That's not an answer," he says, amusement in his voice as he strolls along beside me, his longer legs matching two of my steps with one long stride.

"It's for you. We're checking them out for you." I plant my hands on my hips and turn to face him, irrationally annoyed like I was the other night when we talked about his plans for the future and discovered he had none.

He's eyeing me now like I've lost my mind. Maybe I have. It's not my place to take him on college tours, and I shouldn't be concerned with his future in the first place.

But also...

How can he not have given his future any thought? He has good grades, he's got a great athletic record, and even some extracurriculars, thanks in no small part to his sudden recruitment to our club. But it's like it's never even occurred to him that he might have a future—in college or anywhere else.

I hate that. I hate it even more that no one else in his life had pushed him to think about it. He'd said his parents weren't involved, but surely someone somewhere cared what became of him after high school.

"You want me to look at colleges?" he asks.

I can't tell if he's offended, confused, or touched. He turns away from me before I can tell.

"And check out galleries," I add weakly.

My irritation fades fast as I sneak another sidelong glance in his direction. I haven't offended him, have I?

His expression is still unreadable when he turns back to me with a wry little smile. "All right then." He gestures ahead of him. "Lead the way."

The morning is a success, if I do say so myself.

We didn't have time for the galleries, but we made a plan to tackle them after my interview. But the best part was, I'd been so caught up in talking with Heath, laughing with Heath, figuring out where we needed to go next with Heath—I didn't even have a chance to be nervous about the interview.

Which is for the best. If I overthink it, I know I'll freeze up. So instead, I threw myself into playing tourist with Heath.

We didn't stay long at Columbia, mostly because Heath was so convinced he'd never get in that it felt like a waste of time. We went to the Bronx next, and I'm not sure which one of us loved Fordham University more. I was smitten right off the bat, and I swear I saw Heath's eyes light up when he found out that it was where *The Exorcist* was filmed.

Apparently Heath is a big horror movie fan.

After that, we took a crazy long train ride down to NYU, and that's where we stopped for an early lunch.

"Have you thought about an art degree?" I ask.

He takes a bite of his falafel as we sit side by side on a bench in Washington Square Park. "No," he says simply. He turns to me with a small smile. "But then again, I never really thought much about what I'd get a degree in, if I even went to college."

"You were considering skipping college?"

He nods. "Still might. It seems like an insane amount of money to spend when you don't even know what you want to study."

I nod because...he's not wrong.

"But being here, with you—" He gestures around us at the college kids walking past. His throat works as he swallows. "I'm starting to think. And not just about college."

I tip my head down because I know what he's talking about. He'd said it yesterday too. That being here is making him think about what's next. What comes after Lakeview High. Being away from Lakeview, away from all that's there —including family and exes—that's what has him thinking.

But I can't help but fixate on the way he added *with you*.

It warms my chest and makes my heart clench. Which is stupid. I have nothing to do with his future.

"I never would have thought I was an art guy," Heath says suddenly.

The surprise in his voice makes me laugh. "Why not?"

He shrugs. "I don't know. I play basketball, that's really all I've got going on."

I study his profile. Does he really believe that? "I don't think that's true," I say. "I think basketball is where you found a place to fit in at Lakeview High. But that doesn't mean it's all you are, and it definitely doesn't define who you'll become. People change."

He nods, but I hear my own words and they stick in my brain, playing on a loop. My own words seem to be mocking me, which has me frowning as I crumple up the falafel wrapper and toss it into a nearby garbage.

"We should head back so we're not late for the interview," Heath says.

I nod, inexplicably sad that we're heading back. Which is silly because this interview is why I'm here in the first place. I pull out my phone to check the time and my stomach sinks.

"What's wrong?" Heath asks.

I shake my head. "I don't know. Mr. Deckman called me three times and he texted..." I trail off because I'm too busy calling him back, my stomach twisting into knots of apprehension.

My ringer was off.

Why was my ringer off? How had I not even noticed—

"Celia, where have you been?" Mr. Deckman answers. "I've been trying to reach you for hours."

Hours? My breathing grows shallow as dread pools in my belly.

I hadn't even thought to check my phone because I'd been having so much fun.

"What is it?" I'm already heading toward the subway station, Heath right beside me. "Is it Noelle or—"

"It's the dean," he said. "She wanted to move up your interview because her plans changed and she has to get back to Ithaca."

I stop short.

"Is she..." I draw in a shaky breath. "Did she leave already?"

"I'm afraid so," he says on a sigh.

My throat chokes with tears of frustration. I can't believe this. I missed it. I missed my big opportunity.

And why? My pulse skyrockets as a cold sweat breaks out on my brow.

Because I'd been so caught up in Heath. I'd been too distracted.

I murmur the right things in response to Mr. Deckman's comments about how we'll reschedule for a phone interview, how we'll make this right, how it'll all be okay. But all the while ice is slithering through my veins and my stomach churns with disgust.

I can't believe I let myself get so distracted.

When I hang up, there are tears of frustration and disappointment welling in my eyes.

"Hey." Heath's voice is painfully gentle as he wraps an arm around my shoulder and pulls me in for a hug. "Don't cry."

I cry despite his request. I can't help it.

It's the fact that I missed the interview, but not just that. I know Mr. Deckman is right. I know I can reschedule with a Zoom interview or at least talk to her on the phone. This is not the end of my dream.

I made a good impression and that's what matters.

But I can't shake this overwhelming disappointment.

It's not so much that I missed the interview, but the fact that I let this happen. That's what's really killing me.

I sniff loudly against Heath's shirt, hating how much I love the feel of his arms around me. Cursing myself for the fact that all I want to do is say screw it to the missed interview and let myself revel in this amazing alone time with Heath.

I'm an idiot.

I am such an idiot.

I pull back, out of his arms, glancing away from his kind, concerned gaze.

"I should get back," I say.

"Okay, yeah. Of course. I'll grab us a cab and—"

"No," I say, my tone a little too sharp. "I need to..." I clear my throat and try to soften my voice. "I should go back by myself. I need some time to think."

His eyes widen and I think I see a flicker of hurt, but he nods as he shoves his hands into his pockets and watches me walk away.

I don't want to leave him.

I don't want to be alone right now. I don't want to walk away from Heath and this new connection we've been building. Being with him is exhilarating. It's intoxicating.

Which is exactly why I force myself to take a step back, and then another. "I'll see you at the hotel," I mumble before diving toward the street to hail a taxi.

I get in and give the address—

And I don't look back.

EIGHTEEN

Heath

I AM SUCH AN IDIOT.

Looking around me at the brick buildings and the bustling crowds. I have no idea what I'm doing here.

I am alone in the middle of New York City—and why?

It's amazing how one little change can shift my entire perspective. All morning I'd been overcome with this feeling of how right this all feels. Being here, with Celia, it was like all my life was leading up to this.

And now...

Now I'm wondering how the hell I got it so wrong.

I head toward the subway entrance, past a guy playing a banjo and a food truck that's wafting scents of cinnamon and vanilla.

A minute ago I'd found all these new sights and sounds fascinating, but now it's like I'm pretending to be someone I'm not and I have no idea what I'm doing here.

I'm not the guy who leaves Lakeview for the big city.

I'm not the guy who goes to galleries and art museums and who spends his days touring college campuses.

I run a hand over my hair as I swipe my Metrocard and hop onto the first uptown train I find.

I only half know what I'm doing when the train draws up to the Grand Central stop and I hop out. But as I navigate my way through the crowds, a plan takes shape and, with a quick call to Mr. Deckman, I confirm that it's not the worst idea I've ever had.

And at least it makes me feel like I'm doing something to help Celia. Because I saw the look in her eyes when she was backing away.

I'm part of the reason she'd missed those calls. This is partly my fault. The least I can do is help make this right.

Mr. Deckman assures me he'll reach out to the dean's office to find out if she'll be available tomorrow for an interview, and a few minutes later he texts to tell me it can be arranged.

My muscles unknot a little with relief that at least I'm doing something to cheer Celia up. It doesn't help rid my memory of that look in her eyes when she'd pushed me away, but it's something.

Right now, I'll take it.

With a game plan in place, I head toward the ticket windows but stop short at the familiar blonde in front of me in line. "Pamela?"

She turns with a start at the sound of my voice. Her eyes are red and puffy, and she wraps her arms around herself defensively as she eyes me. "Heath? What are you doing here?"

"I need to book a new ticket," I say. "What about you?"

"Same." She sniffs and looks away. "I hate it here. I'm getting an early train back home."

It's not my problem.

She's not my problem.

And yet... "What happened?"

She mashes her lips together, tears welling in her eyes. "I don't want to talk about it."

I arch my brows. "You sure?"

Her gaze swings back to mine and it's filled with disbelief. "Seriously?"

I blink in surprise at her tone. "What?"

She shakes her head with a huff. "You never want to talk about anything." She throws her hands out wide. "But now that we're broken up you suddenly want to have a talk?"

The harshness in her tone has me jerking my head back, but I know Pamela well enough to know when she's lashing out. Whatever's going on with her, this time it's not about me. Not really. She's upset.

But she's also right. I've never wanted to talk with Pamela. I've always let her rant about her issues with me, and I've said what I've needed to say to smooth things over and make things okay. But we never really talked.

I don't want to be my parents.

Crap. She's right. *I* was to blame for the fact that she and I never talked about anything real. I never tried and I never offered to listen. I never asked what she was thinking and feeling and—

"I was a terrible boyfriend," I say.

She gives a little snort of amusement. "I'm not gonna argue." When I don't respond, she adds grudgingly, "But I wasn't exactly winning awards for girlfriend of the year, either."

We share a look of cynical amusement that ends with us both chuckling.

I nod toward a fast-food pretzel place because the ticket line is starting to move and she and I are in danger of holding it up. "So?" I ask when we're seated. "Want to tell me what happened?"

She purses her lips. "Want to tell me what's going on with you and Celia?"

"Not really, no." I give a huff of laughter and her lips twitch upward before she looks away.

After a long silence, she lets out a loud exhale. "Dominic ended things. Which..." She waves aside my nonexistent protests. "I know what you're thinking. I had it coming. I don't deserve a guy like him, and I know it, it's just..." She trails off, her jaw tightening like she's trying not to cry. "He said I wasn't the girl he'd thought I was and that..." She sniffs. "That hurt."

I don't know what to say so I don't say anything. It gives me no pleasure to see her hurting like this, even if she's hurt me time and again.

"I don't know why I care." She shrugs. "It's so stupid. I don't care what he thinks of me."

But she does. She does care, and that has my heart going out to her. It has me remembering the girl I knew two years ago. The outgoing girl who loved to laugh and have a good time.

The girl I knew before she and I hurt each other so badly.

For all I know, that girl is still in there. I might not see her anymore, but she's there and she's hurting.

Her sigh is so sad it has me looking over at her. "I don't know what's wrong with me."

I reach over and cover her hand with mine. I want to say 'there's nothing wrong with you' but I know what she means and I'm not going to pretend I don't. So instead, I say, "I don't know what's wrong with me either."

She snorts and pulls her hand away. "There's nothing wrong with you, Heath. You're a good guy."

I arch my brows. This is very high praise coming from her, considering the names she's called me in the past. "You think so?"

She rolls her eyes. "I know so." She gives me a small, sad smile. "Why do you think I have such a hard time letting you go?" She looks away, shifting in her seat a bit. "You're nice to me even when I don't deserve it."

"You do deserve it," I say. "You deserve to be treated well."

And as I say it, I realize how badly she needs to hear that. All the crap she's pulled over the years, all the drama and the heartache and even the cheating...

I lean forward and say it again. "You deserve that," I say, firmer this time. "Everybody does."

She nods, but she doesn't look my way. "I don't think Dominic would agree with you."

I flinch, hurt on her behalf. Which is ridiculous, I know. She's just cheated on me. I shouldn't care what Dominic said.

"If he was rude to you—" I start.

She cuts me off with a scoff. "Save the knight-in-shining-armor routine for the girl you actually care about." I blink in surprise but she softens it with a smile. "It's fine, Heath. I'm not jealous and I know I have no right to judge you for moving on." Under her breath, she mutters, "Even if it was really quick."

I start to respond but she moves on, "And besides, Dominic wasn't cruel or anything." She frowns, her gaze distant. "He's a nice guy. What happened wasn't his fault."

I nod. I assumed as much. Poor guy was new to school and unaware of the drama that Pamela loves to create.

"Not that it matters now," she says with a forced breezy tone. "He wants nothing to do with me so..." She shrugs as if she doesn't care.

Neither of us buy it.

"What about you and Celia?" Her eyes gleam with interest, and maybe even a hint of amusement. "I can't believe she finally got the courage to tell you she likes you."

I look away. It feels way too wrong to discuss Celia with Pamela. "We're not together," I say.

"Uh huh," she says. "So you don't like her back?"

I shrug, still looking away. I can't talk to Pamela about this. I just can't.

She scoffs again. "You might be able to convince everyone else you don't have a thing for her, but everyone else doesn't know you the way I do."

I ignore that, my eyes on the line leading to the ticket booth. Will Celia thank me or hate me for stepping in and trying to help?

"Seriously?" Pamela says with a laugh. "You're not gonna admit that you like Celia?"

I can't bring myself to confirm or deny it.

"She doesn't want a relationship," I finally say when the silence stretches too long. I shrug. "And I'm not sure if I'm capable of one anyway."

"Oh please." Pamela sighs. "Don't be such a drama queen."

"I'm not—"

"And don't try to blame this on me," she continues, jabbing a finger in my direction.

I hold my hands up. "I didn't."

She rolls her eyes. "You are totally blaming me, in a roundabout way. I know we had our problems, but don't you dare make it seem like I've ruined you for relationships forever. That's just stupid."

I gape at her. "I didn't say that."

Her lips curve up in a smirk that seems to call me a liar. "We never worked, Heath. We should've stopped trying ages ago."

"But we didn't," I say.

Her gaze meets mine and she doesn't look away.

"Why didn't we?" I ask.

She smiles and it's so bittersweet I'm not sure if she's about to laugh or cry. "I already told you why I kept coming back. You were nice to me, and I knew you'd give me another chance."

I frown at that. "How did you know?"

Her smile grows. "Because you can't help yourself. It's easier for you to take care of other people than worry about yourself. You never think about you and what you want."

I jerk back like I've been struck. "That's not true."

"It is," she says simply. "You're always trying to keep the peace between your parents and make your brothers' feel safe and happy. And with me, well..." That smile turns to a jaded smirk. "I'm the broken toy you can't bear to throw away."

"Cut it out," I say in a low voice. "That's not how I see you."

She arches a brow. "Then you tell me. Why did you keep taking me back when you knew I would only end up hurting you?"

I stare at her for a long moment, and she seems at ease with the silence. She's lost in her own thoughts as well.

She's wrong, though. Maybe I do tend to look after the people I care about, but that's not why I kept taking her back.

I took her back because...because I always knew it would end.

Because you don't have to think about the future with someone when there is no future.

"Pamela," I finally say, leaning in to be sure she's listening. "I never saw you as broken, just...familiar." I shrug helplessly as I search for the right word. "Predictable."

She lets out a sharp laugh. "Ouch."

"Sorry, I didn't mean it like—"

"No, I get it." She waves off my apology. "You were that way for me too. What we had might not have been good, but it was reliable. You were always there when I needed you." She lets out a humorless little laugh as she swipes at her eyes. "You were like some blanky I couldn't get rid of. God, we're so pathetic," she says on a sigh.

I can't help but chuckle at that. "Maybe we *were*, but we don't have to be anymore."

She arches a brow, clearly unconvinced.

"You deserve someone who's nice, Pamela. Someone who loves you for who you are."

She gives me a small smile that's surprisingly sweet. It reminds me of the girl I knew two years ago. "You too, Heath. You deserve that too."

I nod, shifting my chair back because I know now what I have to do. Or at least, I have an idea. Celia might not want a relationship, but it's time I admit that I do.

And it's way past time I go after what I want.

"Hey, Heath?" Pamela says when I go to leave.

"Yeah?"

"Do me a favor." She gives me a small, impish grin. "Don't let your next girlfriend treat you so badly."

I let out a huff of amusement. "I won't."

"Good." She nods for me to leave. "Now go get your girl."

NINETEEN

Celia

"ARE YOU SURE ABOUT THIS?" Noelle asks the next morning over breakfast. "I hate that you're going to miss out on our last day here."

I nod. "I'm sure."

Noelle looks unconvinced, but she doesn't argue.

Mr. Deckman had gotten me an in-person meeting with the dean on campus, but with a five-hour train ride to get there, I have to leave early and miss out on the rest of the fun.

But it's worth it, right? Because this interview is the only reason I'm here.

I frown down at the omelet in front of me in the hotel's dining area. I've been telling myself ever since yesterday afternoon and it still isn't ringing true.

Yes, it's why I wanted to come here, but now that I'm here it doesn't seem as momentous as it had when I was rehearsing my presentation alone in my bedroom back home. Now it feels like I'm in the midst of something bigger.

My mind flashes back to the look on Heath's face just before I walked away and my chest aches.

My emotions are definitely bigger than when I left home. They're bigger than I can handle.

I'm a little afraid they're so big I'll drown in them if given half a chance.

I use my fork to nudge some eggs around on my plate. "I've got to do this, Noelle."

She sighs. "I know."

I told her everything when she got back to the hotel last night. Mara joined in on the conversation too, although we were all a little alarmed that Addie was still MIA.

I know my friends think I'm nuts for sticking with a plan that I made when I was six, but they don't understand what's at stake. Not really.

Addie might have guessed if she'd been on the call, but she wasn't. And I couldn't quite bring myself to tell my two strong, independent besties that I'm terrified of losing myself over Heath.

I couldn't bring myself to say it aloud, so I get that Noelle is confused by my current state of crazy. Any sane person would be.

But that doesn't change the fact that I know what I have to do. And that's to get on the next train to Ithaca with the ticket that Mr. Deckman already arranged for me and tackle this interview as if I'd never been sidetracked.

With one last hug from Noelle, I straighten the skirt of her navy pinstriped dress—the only business casual outfit she owns, she informed me—and I head out the door.

Grand Central is even more of a mad dash than I remembered. Somehow all that grandness feels more overwhelming and less welcoming without Heath standing next to me.

But I don't need him for this leg of the journey. I don't need him at all.

I get on board and claim a seat next to a man engrossed in his iPad and I spend the long trek answering my own hypothetical interview questions, trying to prepare for anything the dean might throw my way.

I have no way of knowing if this is a helpful exercise or not, but at least it keeps me busy.

And it keeps me from checking for messages from Heath. Or pictures of him on social media.

I swear if he and Pamela are back together again, I'll—

Nope. It's none of my business. If Heath wants to continue to spin his wheels in a go-nowhere relationship with a go-nowhere game plan then that is none of my concern.

We'd tried the friends thing and it was a fail.

I'd been right all along, obviously. The only way not to lose my heart and myself was to keep my distance.

When I finally arrive at the college campus, I try to tell myself I'm excited. The campus is lovely, but the truth is, I don't feel that rush of energy like I did in the city. I don't get that buzz of possibility, the appeal of anonymity, that feeling of being lost in something bigger than me.

I like it, though, I tell myself as I finish my self-guided tour and head to the dean's office for my scheduled tour. I like it just fine.

I like the dean too. She's gracious and eloquent, and makes me feel comfortable when she offers me a seat.

"Thank you so much for taking time out of your busy schedule," I say.

"Nonsense." She flashes a brilliant smile. "I had the

pleasure of talking to your teacher yesterday. He told me how disappointed you were that the interview fell through."

"Oh, well—"

"But then when he told me how your boyfriend bought a ticket for you to come here–" She claps a hand over her heart with a sappy smile. "How could I say no to that?"

"My-my what?" I ask.

"Young love," she sighs, her smile widening. "There's nothing quite like it."

"Um..." That's all I've got. Um. The interview of my dreams and I've begun with *um*.

My boyfriend? What is she talking about?

But then she launches into the actual interview and I find myself rattling off my extracurriculars and my classes. She nods politely through it all.

I'm only half paying attention to my own speech, but it's coming out of me by rote, so I suppose all that rehearsing on the train wasn't for nothing. When I come to an end, she crosses her arms and regards me warmly. "You know there's only one question I like to ask prospective students."

I hold my breath, ready for...what? A riddle? Some sort of puzzle?

"What do you want?" she asks.

I blink. "Pardon?"

"What is it that you *want*?" she asks again.

I swallow. "Like, in a school or out of my classes or...?"

She laughs softly, and not unkindly. "Whatever comes to mind. What do you want for your future?"

Everything I've planned for years comes flying to the front of my mind. I know this answer. I want to go to Cornell for undergrad, go on to get my MBA, open my own business by the time I'm thirty, and—

"I don't know."

I stare at her, aghast that *that* is what came out of my mouth.

Even more horrified when I realize that *that* is the truth.

I don't know.

Oh crap. Panic is rising in my chest because—since when do I not know? I've always known what I want in my life.

I planned to live in Disneyworld and be a full-time princess when I was six.

I shove Noelle's thoughts aside. That's not the same thing at all.

The dean leans back in her seat with a satisfied sigh. "That, Ms. Kennedy, is a fantastic answer."

I blink a few times. "Um, it is?"

She nods, her eyes lit with approval. "It is. To be honest..." She shifts so she's leaning forward, resting on her elbows. "It's the kids who think they've got it all figured out who concern me."

My eyes widen. "Really?"

She nods. "They're in for a rude awakening when they realize that the real world doesn't work so neatly as they've planned."

"Oh, that...makes sense," I say.

"Flexibility is key," she says. "The ability to adapt and compromise and keep an open mind." She meets my gaze head-on. "All traits I look for in my students."

I swallow hard as I nod.

I have the feeling that I passed some test. Which would be excellent if I didn't also feel like my head was spinning like...

Well, like that chick from *The Exorcist*.

And now I'm thinking about *The Exorcist*, and Fordham, and the amazing morning I'd had with Heath yesterday when it had felt like anything might be possible.

"I'll look forward to reviewing your application," the dean says as she shakes my hand.

I hadn't even realized we'd both stood, but I have a smile plastered on my face and am saying all the right things.

Again, by rote.

Thank God for long train rides to rehearse.

A few minutes later, I'm back outside in the late afternoon sun. The campus looks pretty as a picture in this light. I know I should head straight back toward the main road to grab a car back to the train station but I find myself standing there on the walkway for way too long, replaying everything the dean had said.

My mind is still reeling from what she'd said about being worried about students too fixated on their plans. I can't even pretend that's not me. Is it possible...?

I look up into the changing leaves of the giant oak tree that towers over me as if some answers might be found there.

Is it possible that in my fear of becoming my mother, I've gone way too far in the other direction? Am I being completely inflexible? Are my plans what I still want or am I just holding onto them because they're my plans?

I rub at my temples with a groan. Again, I can't even pretend I don't already know the answers to those questions.

But other questions are flooding my mind now, and they have my heart racing. My feet finally remember how to work too, and I walk toward the main road as I replay that first part of our conversation.

What boyfriend was she talking about?

What had she meant about a boyfriend...and a train ticket?

I pull out my phone to call for a car and instead find myself calling up Mr. Deckman's contact info.

Me: Hi Mr. Deckman, the interview is over and it went well! How much do I owe you for the last-minute ticket to Ithaca? I'll bring it to school this week.

Deckman: Congratulations! You don't owe me anything. Didn't Heath tell you?

I stop short.

Heath?

What does Heath have to do with this?

With shaking fingers I call for the car, and by the time I get back to the station for my train back to Lakeview a little while later, I'm no closer to understanding what is going on.

I pull out my phone and take a deep breath as I look up Heath's contact information.

The station's getting more and more crowded as the time for departure gets nearer. I should wait until I'm alone. I should wait until—

"Aw, screw it," I mutter.

I hit Heath's number and hold my breath...

"Hello?" His voice alone makes the butterflies in my belly go wild.

"Hey," I say. And then I freeze. What am I supposed to say? *Did you buy me a ticket to Ithaca?* "Um.."

He mutters something that sounds like *hang on* and then the phone goes silent.

I pull it away from my ear and stare at it. Seriously? His phone died again? And *now*?

"Hey." Heath's voice right next to me makes me squeak, and I jump about a foot as I drop my phone.

His smile is sheepish but clearly amused. "Sorry," he says. "I meant to surprise you, not scare the crap out of you."

I smack his arm because I can't speak. Having one's heart in one's throat makes speaking absurdly difficult, I now know. "What are you doing here?" I finally manage.

He rocks back on his heels, his sheepish grin turning to a boyish, hopeful smile that's entirely too cute for life. "I thought maybe you'd want some company on your trip back."

I stare at him in shock.

To be fair, I don't think I've fully recovered from the initial shock of seeing him here. In Ithaca. Five hours away from where I'd left him.

He swallows and glances around before meeting my gaze again. "You never know what can happen with these train rides. It seems like it should be straightforward, but next thing you know your train derails and then you have an outdated schedule and then—"

He stops talking when I throw my arms around his neck. It's sheer instinct that has me holding onto him, holding him tight as my chest tightens with too many emotions at once.

He wraps me up in a hug that makes my heart feel like it might burst and tears spring to my eyes.

He's here. Heath is here...with me.

For me.

"Hi," he says against the top of my head.

I sniff. "Hi."

Greetings complete, we go quiet. But it's not a bad silence. For me it's the silence that comes with not knowing what I want to say.

With not knowing what I *want*. Period.

He strokes one hand over my hair and I close my eyes,

utterly overwhelmed by a warm, fuzzy happiness at being in his arms, surrounded by his scent, pressed up against his chest.

"How'd the interview go?" he asks.

I smile at the sound of his voice through his chest, all low and rumbly and—

And I'm a liar.

"I lied to her," I say, even though I realize a second later that it makes me sound like a lunatic.

"You *lied?*" Amusement laces his voice like he's waiting for me to tell him a funny story.

But I did lie to the dean.

She'd asked me what I want and I'd said I don't know. But I do.

To deny it is so crazy stupid.

I want *this*.

I wrap my arms tighter around Heath and he hugs me harder in response.

I want *Heath*.

TWENTY

Heath

I LOVE CELIA'S HUGS.

I grin as I bury my face in her hair and breathe her in.

Her hugs are so perfectly her. They're impulsive and sweet. They're unabashedly caring. Her hugs speak louder than words, and I'm pretty sure right now her hug means she's happy that I'm here.

Even if she hasn't said so.

When the train pulls up, we get on and grab our seats. We haven't really said much at all, but the fact that she's not pissed that I'm here gives me hope.

"How'd the interview go?" I ask again.

She peeks over at me as she nibbles on her lower lip. She looks so lost in thought I'm almost sorry I interrupted whatever is going on in that head of hers. Finally, she nods. "Good," she says. "I think it went well."

"But you lied?" I ask.

She sort of chokes on a laugh and gives her head a little

shake. But it's the way her cheeks start to turn pink that makes me really curious.

"Forget I said that," she says.

One side of my mouth hitches up in a smile. "Fair enough."

She laughs softly like I said something funny. "How do you do that?"

I arch my brows. "Do what?"

She leans back against the window as the train starts to move. "How are you so easy about everything? I mean, you seem so content to just...go with the flow."

I arch my brows in surprise. Am I? "I guess I never thought of myself like that."

I think of all the times I've been called brooding or angsty over the past couple years, but I never thought of myself like *that* either.

She tilts her head to the side as she studies me. "That's one thing I've always loved about you. You're so thoughtful, but so at ease with everything all the time. You're like some Buddhist monk in a teen boy's body."

I burst out in a laugh so loud half the car turns to look at me.

Celia's grinning at me, and I'm—oh crap, I am *happy*. I am so freakin' happy it hurts.

I can't hold it back any longer and the words come tumbling out. "I like you, Celia."

She blinks and then her eyes widen. I reach for her hand because I'm a little terrified that she's going to pull away.

"I know I said this already, so it's not exactly news, but I really do like you, and—" I stop to take a deep breath. "And I want to be with you."

She blinks a few times in response.

Well, at least that wasn't a no...right?

I squeeze her hand and shift in my seat so I'm fully facing her. "I know I have a bad history when it comes to relationships, but I don't want to let that stop me from trying. If I did—If I just kept repeating my mistakes and never tried for more, then...then..."

I don't finish, but she nods all the same, and I know she gets it.

I'd be just like my parents.

"I might not be the perfect boyfriend, but I want to try," I say. "With you."

Her eyes well with tears, and my heart does a dip and weave motion that leaves me feeling a little ill.

Crying is probably not a good sign. Is it?

I hurry on before she can speak because I'm not about to let this moment pass without saying everything that needs to be said. I'm terrifyingly aware that this might be my only chance. "I know that you're scared of relationships," I say. "And I get it. I really do. But the thing is...you don't trust yourself."

She presses her lips together, tears starting to spill over. But she still doesn't speak.

I swallow hard. "I wish you would," I say. "I think you *should*. But until you do, I'm asking you to trust me instead."

Her brows hitch up in surprise. "You...you what?"

I lean in toward her, trying to block out the view of the rest of the train so all she sees is me. Because honestly, that's how I've been feeling for the past forty-eight hours. Like all I see is Celia and everything she brings into my life.

Laughter. Passion. New ideas. Thoughts of the future...

It's like Celia tore down some wall I hadn't even known I was hiding behind. And now that it's down, I can't go backwards. There's only moving forward from here on out, and I hope like hell it will be with Celia at my side.

"I want you to trust me," I say again, feeling only slightly less idiotic as I repeat myself. Why should she trust me when she doesn't trust herself? I don't know. But I need her to know that I get it. That I get *her*.

I take her other hand in mine as well so I'm gripping them both as I meet her gaze. "Celia Kennedy, I hereby solemnly vow, I will not let you make any decisions based on me."

Her lips part, and for a second I can't breathe as I wait for her response.

Then her eyes start to warm and her lips start to twitch, and the terrifying silence is broken with her light laughter. "What if I want to?" she asks, her brows drawing together in feigned confusion as her eyes sparkle with laughter.

"Nope," I say as I try not to smile. "I won't allow it."

"You might not have a choice," she says.

My head dips as a laugh escapes. She's kidding. I know she's only teasing. And the fact that she can make a joke about this right now floods me with renewed hope.

I lift my head to find her gaze unfocused like she's lost in thought. "What are you thinking about?" I ask quietly.

She takes a deep breath and glances out the window. "I liked it here. At Cornell, I mean."

"Oh. Okay." I nod, some of that hope faltering. Here I'd been opening a vein and spilling my heart out, and she's...thinking about her interview.

She turns back to me, her gaze focused now. Focused and...resolved. "I liked it, but I didn't love it. Not the way I thought I would."

I have no idea how I'm supposed to respond, so I don't.

"I always thought I had it all figured out," she continues. "I always thought I knew what I wanted…"

She's quiet for a moment, like she's still stewing over her next words. I swallow down a wave of nerves. "That's funny," I say. "Because I never knew what I wanted. But now I do."

Her gaze lifts to meet mine.

"I want you," I say. Just in case that wasn't abundantly clear already.

Her lips start to curve up again in a hesitant smile. "Just me?"

I shrug. "The rest I'll figure out as I go."

"Figure it out as you go, huh?" Her tone is teasing and that makes my chest warm with affection.

"Not a good plan?"

She gives a rueful laugh. "Probably way better than mine. I was so sure I had it all figured out. But now…" She exhales loudly. "Now I feel like I don't know anything anymore."

I nod because I can totally get that. "Maybe—" I start and stop as I think through my next words. "Maybe you don't need to know everything. Maybe you don't even have to know what comes next." I reach out to brush her hair back because I'm dying for an excuse to touch her, to be closer. "Maybe for right now it's enough to just know who you are."

The look in her eyes is heart-achingly vulnerable. "And who's that?"

I smile, my chest tightening with affection. This girl's confidence was shaken, but I know for a fact she won't be down for long. "You're someone who's smart and strong, thoughtful and passionate, beautiful and driven…"

Her smile trembles a bit, and a fresh round of tears fill her eyes.

"I know who you are," I say. "But more importantly, I know who you are not."

"What's that?" she asks in a voice choked with tears.

"You are *not* someone who would lose herself over some guy. You are not someone who'd give up on her dreams for anyone, and definitely not for some guy." After a beat, I add, "No matter how epically hot this guy might be."

She gives a cute little teary giggle at my teasing. "He *is* pretty hot," she agrees.

I smile, but my heart is racing with nerves. She hasn't said yes yet, and I'm starting to understand why people have nightmares about being naked in front of their whole class. That's pretty much exactly how I feel right now. Absolutely naked. Like my insides are on full display.

"Before," she starts hesitantly. "When I'd said I'd lied to the dean?"

I nod, trying not to hold my breath.

"She'd asked me what I want. Just point blank. *What do you want?*" She shakes her head like she's still amazed by that. "I told her I didn't know. But I lied."

My heart is slamming against my ribcage now, and I'm afraid I'm crushing her hand in mine. I ease my grip as I inhale.

"I don't know if I still want to go to Cornell. I don't know if I want to get an MBA. I'm not sure I know much of anything when it comes to the future, but I do know one thing that I want right now." She leans in toward me, her brown eyes so warm and deep a guy could drown in them. "I want to be with you."

My heart lurches and my chest swells. I don't even think before I reach for her, cupping her cheek with one hand while my other arm wraps around her and drags her close.

Her sigh is sweet as my lips close over hers.

This. This right here is what I've been dreaming about. Had I really thought I could just be Celia's friend after knowing how good it feels to kiss her and hold her in my arms?

Her arms loop around my neck as she tilts her head to the side, giving me access as she teases me with these innocent little kisses that remind me that I need to take things slow. For both our sakes.

I don't want to repeat any of my past mistakes, and that means being open and honest with this girl every step of the way. It means talking as well as kissing. It means giving her time and space so she doesn't feel like she's drowning.

One of us ought to have their head above water. And as I claim her lips in another slow, achingly tender kiss, I know one thing for certain—it has to be her.

Because...me?

I'm already a goner.

TWENTY-ONE

Celia

MARA'S GOT my back when we walk into Lakeview High on Monday morning.

Not that I need backup, but...I sort of do.

"You have nothing to be nervous about," Mara says, laughter lacing her tone.

I smile and nod because I know she's right. It's stupid that I'm this nervous. It's not like my whole world has changed. I just have a boyfriend now.

Heath Reilly is my boyfriend.

My lungs hitch the way they always do when I think about that.

Heath Reilly is my boyfriend.

This is good news, not something to freak out about. And yet...

Ever since he left my house last night after a ridiculously hot goodnight kiss, it started. The fears, the worries, the nerves.

Not that I'm doubting my decision.

I'm not.

It's just...

"I don't know how to be someone's girlfriend," I admit in a whisper.

Mara rolls her eyes. "No one knows how until they're in a relationship. And it's not like learning to drive, Celia. You don't need to pass a test or learn a new set of skills. You'll figure it out as you go."

I nod, a smile tugging at my lips because all I can picture is Heath's nonchalant expression and those gorgeous hazel eyes of his when he said *the rest I'll figure out as I go.*

How is that so easy for everyone else? For me, figuring things out as I go still sounds terrifying.

"Have you heard from Addie yet?" I ask as we turn down the crowded hallway to our lockers.

Mara nods. "She finally texted me back yesterday to say she'll be back in school today."

"Oh good."

"You know that means you're going to have to tell her the whole story the second you see her." Mara claps her hands together in a totally un-Maralike squeal. "She's not going to believe you're finally dating Heath Reilly!"

"Shhhh." I snag her arm and pull her over toward my locker. "Do you have to scream it to the world?"

She rolls her eyes. "Newsflash, Celia. Everyone is going to know by the end of the day if they don't already." She arches her brows, her eyes lit with excitement. "Heath Reilly and Celia Kennedy, the hot new couple? This is huge news."

"Not as big as the great Ryan and Mara romance that shocked the nation," I tease.

She laughs. "Nope, this is bigger. I don't think anyone thought Heath would ever move on from that toxic dump that was his last relationship, and no one would have guessed that you, my sweet and wonderful friend, would finally woman up and snag him."

"I didn't snag him," I mumble. "That makes me sound like I'm a cavewoman who hit him over the head and dragged him back to my cave."

Mara smirks. "All right, fine. You wooed him. You made him swoon. You won his heart. You—"

"Enough." I hold up a hand, but we're both laughing at her ridiculousness. I hear a ding from my phone announcing a new text and dig my phone out of my purse.

Noelle: Don't you dare cause any more gossip until I get back.

Mara laughs as she reads over my shoulder. "It must be killing her to be stuck on a train back to the city while you and Heath are making your big debut."

I huff. "Would you cut it out? You're not helping my nerves. Like, at all."

"Sorry not sorry," Mara says with an evil little grin.

I set one hand on my locker door as I turn back to face her. "And we're not making any *debut*. We're just going to school today, like we always do."

"Uh huh." Mara's outright laughing at me now.

I open my mouth to continue my argument, but Addie's sudden arrival at my side has me forgetting all about Mara's teasing. She's wearing a flowing, flowery dress that is so perfectly Addie and she's beaming at me with a brilliant smile. "Miss me?"

"Addie! We missed you so much." I throw my arms around her in a big hug that she returns with a happy little squeak.

"Is it true?" she asks. "Please tell me it's true."

I pull back, my cheeks inexplicably warming. These are my friends. I should not be blushing. But Addies' wide-eyed look of excitement has my heart tripping all over the place as it hits me smack in the face as if for the first time.

Heath Reilly is my boyfriend.

The guy I've liked from afar for a lifetime likes me back.

It still feels unreal.

Heck, it felt surreal even when Heath was kissing me on the train, and when we were holding hands and cuddling on the way home, talking about everything and nothing as the hours flew by.

It hadn't stopped feeling surreal, not even when he gave me a ride to my still-empty house and lingered over the world's longest, sexiest, and most delicious goodbye.

I sigh now at the memory, and that has my two friends exchanging knowing smirks.

"I'll take that as a yes," Addie says.

I nod. "We're official."

Even if I can't quite believe it.

"But what about you?" I ask Addie. "How was your week in Montana?"

"It was...good."

Her slight pause is enough to have me and Mara exchanging a worried look.

"Addie," Mara says slowly. "Is everything okay?"

She nods. "Yeah." When we continue to stare at her in clear disbelief, she shrugs. "There's some stuff going on, but I don't really want to talk about it right now." Her smile brightens, and if it's a little forced, neither Mara nor I call her on it. Addie will talk when she's ready. Like Heath, she's thoughtful like that. Sometimes she needs time to think things through before she can talk about it.

She edges closer, giving me a side hug, her bright red hair brushing against my cheek. "Besides, I'd much rather hear all the details of all I missed while I was gone."

"Well, in that case..." I draw in a huge inhale, ready to start from the very beginning, but I'm cut short by the first bell.

We only have a few minutes to grab our things and get to homeroom.

"At lunch," I promise Addie. "I'll catch you up on all the details."

"You'd better," she says.

Mara snags Addie's arm and starts dragging her away, giving a pointed look over my shoulder. "We'll just be going now," she says, laughter in her voice.

Addie's eyes widen, and that's when I realize what's going on. Sure enough, I spin around to see Heath heading toward me, a lazy smile spread across his handsome features and his gaze trained on me.

My heart leaps, and I swear it feels like fizzy bubbles are floating through my bloodstream.

"Morning." Heath leans against the locker next to mine, his smile crooked and his eyes warm with tenderness.

My lungs falter in the face of this look. Butterflies go nuts in my belly.

"Hey," I say. My cheeks are turning to flames again, and I can't even say why.

I wasn't nervous around Heath yesterday when he was kissing me and holding my hand and snuggling me on a train. But here I am, tongue-tied and frazzled all over again.

He arches his brows, amusement dancing in his eyes. "Are we still good?"

I nod.

His eyes narrow a bit. "You're not having second thoughts, are you?"

I shake my head. Oh, this is ridiculous. I know how to speak around Heath Reilly. "I'm just nervous," I blurt out. "I don't know why. It's stupid."

His grin is slow and lethal. I swear he could stop my heart with that smile. Actually, he *does* make it stop, and when it starts again, it's racing at doubletime.

"It's not stupid." He leans in a little and lowers his voice. "I'm a little nervous too."

That makes me smile and some of my anxiety ebbs. "Yeah?"

He nods. "This is new to me too."

I open my mouth, ready to remind him that it's not the same. He's been in a relationship, even if it was a bad one. Not to mention, he hasn't spent a decade crushing on me from afar. But he continues before I can speak.

"I'm happy," he says. The flicker of awe in his eyes as he says it makes my heart turn to mush. He reaches for me and tugs me close. "I'm happy, and I don't want to mess this up."

And just like that, the nerves morph into excitement. Anticipation. Maybe even love.

Heath Reilly is my boyfriend—and I am the luckiest girl in the world.

"You can't mess this up," I say as I press a palm to his chest, directly over his heart.

"Oh no?" He arches a brow.

I shake my head. "I won't let you."

He laughs under his breath, and I know he's remembering the promise he made in the train. He won't let me make the mistakes I fear the most. The least I can do is promise him the same.

He nods. "Deal."

He leans in slowly, like he's afraid I'm gonna freak out, but when his lips touch mine, I forget all about my nerves. My hands curl into his T-shirt, and I lean into him just as he deepens the kiss.

His lips are hot and firm, his breath warm against my skin. His scent wraps around me and makes me dizzy as my heart flutters with pure happiness.

The second bell has us pulling apart, and if people are staring, I can't bring myself to care.

Right now there's just us, and we are good.

We are better than good.

"What now?" I ask.

"Now I walk you to class," he informs me.

I laugh. "Wow. You really are chivalrous, you know that?"

He lifts one shoulder in a shrug. "Do you mind?"

I shake my head as I go to open my locker door. "I love it."

The second the locker door opens, I gasp. Paper is falling at my feet. I kneel down to pick up the stacks that had fallen and find that...it wasn't just paper.

It was cards.

It was homemade Valentine's Day cards. I stare at the cheesy heart cutout in my hands with wide eyes as my pulse hammers in my ears. For a second, I think maybe I've lost my mind. That I'm dreaming, at the very least.

Heath squats down beside me, his gaze searching my face. "Too much?"

The noise that slips out is part gasp, part laugh, and all joy. "You are crazy."

He laughs, his grin unrepentant. "About you? Yes. Guilty."

I'm shaking my head in disbelief as he helps me to stand. "I can't believe you did that for me."

"You said that's the one thing you'd been missing." He glances down at the pile at my feet. "I figure I had some years to make up for."

I start to laugh, and then I can't stop.

He's chuckling too as he pulls me into his arms and kisses the top of my head. "Come on," he says at last when the halls start to clear. "We'd better get you to homeroom."

I look down at the pile of cards. "I need to clean these up first."

"I'll come back and pick them up," he says.

"I can help—"

"Oh no," he interrupts, only partially teasing. "You are not going to be late. Not on my account."

My heart squeezes because I know he means it. He's going to keep his promise come hell or high water, and I love that about him. I love that so much.

Because he's right. I can trust him. And maybe one day soon I'll be able to trust myself not to follow in my parents' footsteps. But for now...

For now, I am overcome with gratitude that this guy likes me as much as I like him.

I shake my head, going up on tiptoe to pull his head down to meet mine. "I'm not going to be late for you," I say. My lips quirk up in a smile as they brush over his.

"*This?*" I kiss him again, harder this time and with all the love that's in my heart. "This is for me."

EPILOGUE

Two weeks later...

CELIA

HEATH'S ARMS are wrapped around my waist, and for the second time in as many weeks, I'm burrowed inside his hoodie. "It's not even winter yet," I complain. "How is it so cold?"

His arms tighten and he lowers his head to kiss a spot at the base of my neck.

I shiver again, but this shiver has nothing to do with the cold.

"Better question." I swear I can hear the smile in his voice. "Why are you perpetually underdressed?"

I pull my head back to look up at him, and he widens his eyes in feigned innocence. "I'm not complaining," he says quickly. "I benefit nicely from this arrangement."

I laugh as I rest my head back against his chest. "I probably should have known that the lake would be windy." And we both know I have a sweater in his car somewhere. But we've both agreed, body heat is far more efficient.

He kisses the top of my head in response. "At least you don't have to go swimming in an ice cold lake," he says.

I wince as I pull back to see that—yup. Mara and Ryan are doing it. Well, they're psyching themselves up to do it. They've stripped down to their swimsuits and are about to dive into the lake, which has gone from refreshingly chilly to ice cold as the summer weather gave way to fall.

"I can't believe they're doing all these stupid stunts to win a scavenger hunt," Noelle says. She's standing beside us, her lightweight track jacket zipped up to her nose.

"I can," Elijah says. "Those two will compete over anything."

"But they're on the same team," Addie says. Her nose is crinkled up in confusion as she stuffs her hands into the pockets of her ankle-length skirt. She has a thing for skirts with pockets.

"That only makes them worse," I say.

I feel Heath's nod of agreement.

The scavenger hunt has become an obsession for some seniors—not us, though. Heath and I have been too caught up in our newfound couple happiness to pay much mind to it. But when we found out that Mara and Ryan were tackling this challenge today and needed someone to capture it in photos, we couldn't resist coming to watch.

It seems we weren't alone.

"Does anyone actually have their phone to take pictures?" Leah asks.

Elijah's cousin is snuggled up to her boyfriend Ben as they try to shelter from the wind too.

We all exchange looks trying to see who has the camera.

"You guys!" Mara's dancing from one foot to the other, her teeth chattering as Ryan tries to warm her from behind with his bare arms. "Somebody get their phone out before I freeze to death."

Everyone hustles into action and Noelle is the first to have her camera out and ready. "Okay, go for it," she calls.

I wince and burrow further into Heath for warmth as I watch my crazy friends dive into the ice-cold water.

"They're insane," Heath says in that mild way of his that never fails to make me laugh.

"Totally nuts," I agree.

Once Noelle's done taking pictures and Mara and Ryan are back on shore shivering together under a ton of towels and blankets, the rest of us go back to talking.

"Who's going to be around this weekend?" Elijah asks.

"Why?" Noelle shoots back. "Another party at your place?"

Elijah's cocky grin is the only answer we need.

"I'll be there," Noelle says easily.

"Us too," Leah chimes in.

Everyone looks to us and I shake my head. "Sorry, we're going on a road trip."

"Road trip!" Elijah shouts, pumping a fist like a dork. Noelle swats his hand down.

"We're checking out some colleges," Heath explains.

Noelle turns to me with her brows drawn down. "I thought you had your heart set on Cornell."

I shrug. "I'm exploring my options."

Heath nods. "And she's helping me figure out where I might want to apply."

"Aw," Leah croons. "You guys are going to school together?"

"No," Heath says quickly.

I smother a laugh. "Not necessarily," I add.

"Not unless it's what we each want irregardless of the other," Heath says. His tone is so official, it makes me giggle.

We've been talking about this a lot lately, and Heath takes his vow so seriously that he's gone a little over the top. The second the conversation and the attention turns from us, he turns to me with an arch look. "I mean it," he says. "I'm not even going to tell you where I'm applying."

I shrug. "Fine."

"Fine."

He cracks first, a grin tugging at his lips as he leans down and steals a kiss. "Have I mentioned lately how much I'm looking forward to another trip with you?"

I laugh. "Just a few hundred times."

He opens his mouth to respond, but Addie's joined us and chimes in. "Maybe you guys can take a road trip to Montana sometime soon."

"That would be awesome," Heath says easily, but something in Addie's tone has me stiffening and pulling away from Heath...well, as much as his hoodie allows.

"Are you going back for another visit?" I ask.

Addie's smile looks strained. "Sort of." She licks her lips and glances around as the rest of our friends join in on the conversation. It's like everyone can sense her tension and she's the center of attention. "Um, actually...the truth is...I'm moving there."

"What?" Mara's gasp is only slightly interrupted by her chattering teeth, and Ryan wraps an arm around her as he frowns at Addie.

"You're leaving Lakeview?"

Addie nods, her cheeks pinkening at all the attention. "I don't want to be...well, it's a long story. But it's for the best."

"I can't believe you're transferring senior year," I start.

But I clamp my mouth shut when I see Addie's eyes start to sparkle with unshed tears. The last thing she needs is me pointing out how much it sucks that she'll be missing out on senior year memories.

Heath's arms tighten around me as if he can feel my surge of sadness and is trying to comfort me.

"Of course we'll come visit you, Addie," Heath says. He looks down at me with such understanding and affection, it takes my breath away. "Won't we, Cece?"

He's been calling me that more and more when we're alone together and right now it's like a reminder that he's here, that I'm loved. It gives me the strength I need to force a smile for Addie's sake.

"Of course we will," I say.

Everyone else starts talking and asking questions, trying to reassure Addie as we get the full story.

Heath leans down in the midst of it all, his low voice close to my ear. "I'm already looking forward to a cross country trip with you."

I smile up at him as I go on tiptoe to claim a kiss. "That sounds like heaven."

THANK YOU FOR READING! If you enjoyed the story, a review would be most appreciated. Missed Mara & Ryan's story? You can find it in *Just One Kiss*. Stay tuned for Addie's story next in *One Little Lie*!

ABOUT THE AUTHOR

MAGGIE DALLEN IS a big city girl living in Montana. She writes romantic comedies in a range of genres including young adult, historical, contemporary, and fantasy. An unapologetic addict of all things romance, she loves to connect with fellow avid readers. Subscribe to her newsletter at http://eepurl.com/bFEVsL

Made in the USA
Monee, IL
09 August 2024